Napoleon's Mare

Napoleon's Mare

A Novella by Lou Robinson

FICTION COLLECTIVE TWO

Boulder • Normal

Published by Illinois State University and Fiction Collective Two with support given by Illinois State University President's Discretionary Fund, the Publications Center of the University of Colorado at Boulder, the National Endowment for the Arts, the Illinois Arts Council, and the Illinois State University Fine Arts Festival.

Address all inquiries to Fiction Collective Two, c/o English Department, Illinois State University, Normal, Illinois 61761.

Napoleon's Mare
 Lou Robinson
First edition
First printing, 1991.

ISBN: 0-932511-47-3 (cloth)
ISBN: 0-932511-48-1 (paper)

Manufactured in the United States of America
Distributed by the Talman Company
Typesetting and design by Carol Friedman, Gail Gaboda, and Jean Lee

Some of the writing in this collection originally appeared in the following journals:

"Moving Objects at a Distance" and "World Wars Might Happen," *Epoch* 40, No. 1 (1991, Ithaca, NY)
"A Lesbian Is a Memoir," *Tessera* 9 (1990, Ontario)
"Rapport," *Trivia* 16/17 (1990, Montague, MA)
"Changing Sides," "Forward Desire," and "Sound Worry," *Trois* 6, No. 1 (1990, Quebec)
"How Death Was Overset with Yes," *f(Lip)* 3, No. 1 (1989, Vancouver)
"Fort Ancient," *Frontiers* 10, No. 3 (1989, Boulder, CO)
"Bernadette" and "Eleanor," *Paragraph* 4 (1988, Holyoke, MA)
"Adelle," *Praxis* (1981, Ithaca, NY)
"I'm in the bathroom cutting up her shoes," "Studying what is close at hand," and "Opaque dust lane," *Chiaroscuro* 2 (1980, Ithaca, NY)

Contents

Napoleon's Mare

a novella

I Make Balance

But that doesn't stop me. The train fills up with smoke, the lights go out, the tunnel screams and some launch themselves out onto a darker ledge, but that didn't turn her around. How can you suffer so much when you know so little? So you think you know more? What do you know? The thud of such sentences, that kind of drama, that long ago.

Last night a deer came and spoke at the foot of the stairs. What stairs I heard you say and then I lost her words. She spoke of the kind of food she wanted, she looked up the dark green walls imploring and familiar. She knew me, she showed this naked hunger nowhere else. What should I feed her, what did she say? The best I can always, never enough, never can find the right shape for the words. I know a lot of things I can't express.

In the zone of beginnings, where color is deep, and matter transcended, a body remembering a touch is made light just walking over a bridge...grows irritated by memory scraping her cells. Why does everybody talk about the body? All the best states leave it behind. It is a launching pad, a jetty. Can you really say sensation begins and ends with the body? Sex, can you say you had it confined? You can't fill

your cells with undemanding love, no matter how steady
your learned breath, and honor the body. What is this
planet worship, green like dollars? Mindfulness. Rightful
disposal of an inch of plastic. While we wreck each other,
talk like tanks, rebound like heads on rubber.

I am meanwhile mindful of that sinister man from Florida,
his long grey ponytail, utterly sinister, his too straight
posture for a drunk, dangerous. Destitution hasn't suffi-
ciently humbled him. He neither believes nor disbelieves
that the world will turn upside down. By the angle of his
wrist I know that he has killed people. No doubt a proper
response. But I don't want to be the meat for his knife. I am
mindful of everything, the bunch of gull feathers protruding from a styrofoam cup on the tracks, one blue sock
gummed to a puddle of train oil. In these I read the demise
of the planet I love, an ordinary day. I wait for the truly
revelatory sign, someone giving something without looking terrified.

I put two ibis next to a dog with its ears wrapped in gauze.
The dog in gauze—against a stone wall, Maine? Italy? This
will guarantee passage to a place of peace. You have to be
vigilant. Blood, wailing, pictures of burning must be coun-
tered with those that soothe. But too many happy scraps lull
you into idiocy, victimdom. Keep looking. I make balance.
You illustrate your passage ahead of you. You carve it. The
man from Florida is all the way dead, from killing, or the
other way around. Either you go numb and the mad takes
a plan of its own or you pay tribute to pictures, surfaces,
homage even. You worship. I like this, it smacks of the snake
church in Columbus, Ohio. No I hate it. Holy, that would be.
No. Smother religiousity. The dead man from Florida
thinks he is holy. He has his followers. He is out this sunny

day taking his followers for a walk. I paste a giraffe next to a sandstone arch.

I throw out all pictures of human bodies, remembering how much I loved love. So many twisting wrenching wringing sweats, the sheen that illumines objects, bridges, coffee, speeding, with wonder always that unearthly shade of blue. In my sleep the letters realign becoming vole. A soft smoky taupe creature, blind, with claws. On the same page a white horse with hair to the ground stands still against a tapestry of embroidered Russian shirts. On its back a panther lolls in the detachment of the third sphere.

The horse with the longest mane in the world was stuffed and pulled through the streets of Delaware, Ohio, every fourth of July. Then she would make us rum and Coke, my best friend Nan. Both thirteen, lying together in boy pajamas our manes to the ground she tells me Paul McCartney has just fallen against me in the dark of the London cab, she demonstrates. Below us her dog chews a mouthful of rubber bands with more abandon. She would tell me later she was not that way. The words people use. That way. Little experiment. Really special.

In a bedroom all yellow and black, like his poisonous scent, Jean Naté, the new boy tells me that his father is working late at the bowling alley. That red hair is really special. Considerate for seventeen—Vaseline, condoms. Washing the sheets after, quick before the parents come home from the bowling alley. Tenderly two smooth hairless bodies, so similar so breastless, breathless with pride and embarrassment, relief, got rid of it. It wants back in periodically, whatever it was. Sometimes taking the shape of little children, unwanted, sent on their way, mistaken misbegotten. It wants a shape

to have a mouth to have a voice. The thing for which I staked
no claim. Stook. Stood my ground but always despite. Took
nothing. In spite of. Confusing spite for spirit, that which
refuses that which rises again to reach out. Hard to name it
when it has never had a future or a past. In the presence of
that moment when, children really, my best friend became
my lover in the process of becoming a lover of men, that
thing that stopped speaking nevertheless I cherish it, despite its silencing, because it loved anyway, unjudging. No
one will know, unless I tell them, that this white ibis whose
neck bows in—vanity, and out—terror, is Clay, a gay blond
boy from Fort Wayne, Indiana, who once played Pan in
Oberlin, Ohio, covered in glue and teal blue sequins.

If I had so many then I am qualified to say—forsake the
body. Don't you think you all grow old? What do you think
it means but decay and imprisonment? It's only given as an
obstacle, like parents, like fences to a yearling, to be rushed,
battered, flung over to freedom. Yes, to the liberty of pasting
animals cut from the National Geographic onto newsprint.
So they can express themselves.

A crane emits a line of type: "Witnesses say both men took
shelter under a tree and lightning struck the tree, causing
both men to fall to the ground unconscious." shelter. struck.
I am Maat, I make balance.

"The men were overcome by smoke. Sometimes they can
chop a hole to release it. But not in vinyl siding." I slap down
a grieving African elephant cut from its graveyard of bones.
sometimes. overcome.

And see a boy bring a jellyfish out on a plastic shovel when.
I'm not saying when because of the bewilderment that is

our real condition. Another thing ending in that sunny way they have. Next to me, the woman I was trying to love is busy burning a red oval between two black crossed straps. Iron-shaped or alcove shaped. Reading as she burns reducing Virginia Woolf to a sum of abuse. Sorrel (a strawberry roan knee-deep in the green herb of the same name—an utterly ill-suited name) stops reading, facing away, says: "Then we shouldn't continue this little experiment. Since you press. I can't give you what you want." Sorrel, earlier, prancing like a saddlebred in the crusty night waves to invisible applause from a row of beach chairs. Gritty heels on the bed watching the young James Mason on the motel tv. The mystery of affections. As if they can be bundled, thrown into the sun in a quivering transparent mass. Who could stand to touch it? Better to say I can't take you in. Eyes greener than the water behind them, taking her in. Spitting her out. Was it her neck I thought I wanted, the greying forelock curl (a dapple-grey Connemara), the pieces, shattered, I wanted the pieces. I wanted to put them back together for her. I wanted her to take me apart. There's more ego than love in this, they said. They said, you want her to pay? What coin? They, well, they sounded like me, but I didn't listen.

The man who every time his eye fell on the word death in the newspaper had to search until he found the word love.

The man who this the man who that. I kill a couple more with glue and lightning.

The woman who glued her boyfriend's lips together with Crazyglue. Who shot her husband and left a note saying she'd rendered him back to his maker. Maker. I make balance. For every woman tearing at another woman, seeing her own ugliness, seeing her end, pushing it away, I find a line in type about men dying violently, thus I make balance. Words are everything. Once there were bodies but they only house an inner voice. And it lies, to bolster its crumbling shelter. Anybody can find tragedy in the newspaper. Search your own heart, I tell myself. But self-pity is so immobilizing. I note my big left toe is turning white. I can only find vengeance enough to rise from the black antiseptic ink of the daily papers.

I never said you shouldn't try to describe the earth, the flesh you encounter, you run aground. What good is a thought without a body to test it? Writing requires a hand. No, I'll do it all mental. But the man from Florida is exactly that unconnected. He never makes anything. Other men come, swarm to give him things, cigarettes, drink, a blanket, a red vest. "Give give give," Sorrel toasted, raising a piece of her grandmother's crystal, imitating her Danish uncle summarizing the perfect marriage. Murder must be holy. Women give to men, men give to men. Women, what they give to each other is torn from bloody roots.

The man from Florida tells them he's part Cree, but I know that he is the son of two Scottish miners from West Virginia, he never had a mother. The heat makes me oracular. So hot the glue shines through the paper. Why do crazy people wear so many clothes? Because where else are they going to put them? There he is taking his posture for a walk, taking his wardrobe for une promenade.

In hotels Sorrel would immediately put her clothes in drawers, even if only for a night, one here, one there, saying, "I like little spaces, the apartment I grew up in was a coliseum." Some people try to occupy space. I always tried to give the impression of imminent departure. Looking backwards was the problem. Problem, I write across the face of a gnu glued over a story about walking for peace. "Walking for a more livable world…people are using many strategies to free themselves…the fee is $3,000…makes it easier for the upper middle class…but one big component is…a celebration…of diversity."

Problem. I underline, so no one will mistake me for a Buddhist.

"Firefighters pumped more than 18,000 gallons of water onto the lava flow in a futile attempt to save the temple. Meanwhile the world's most active volcano continued to pump out half a million cubic meters." Next to these lines I glue a tree frog an impossible shade of green suctioned onto a window of newsprint through which it can now read about hot and cold. Pump. "Pump me from behind," Sorrel would say, "It turns me on."

I loved it when she leaned across like that, a deep breath, go. Over her coffee steaming toward her face everything streams toward her when she gets this way. She was saying bridle path. While everyone else was mumbling about the dusty death of the earth. That has such phrases in it. I'm in her present breath, each word. I can't enfold myself in their despair. On her tooth I see the sacred marriage of a woman and a horse. The restraining rein. The way they both give with ardent forward leaning at the pressure of my knee. How they learn to love to jump even with lips around a piece of steel. Embracing contradiction with more heart than all our best intentions. Always warm it first with my breath. Why here, now? To lean like that over her coffee reading urgently. I'm sick of service, succor, salvation.

Reining in. Saving no one, not a hair on her head. Say she simply loves to run and with me on her back, not a solitary pleasure, she wants to give me speed to feel me press more more. Restrain me. I'm forgetting we are here to witness and to mourn. No, the heart of this beast is here to surge, give it rein. Standing weaving crazily on her back, dropping to her mane just at the door before decapitation.

Now I'm keeping Sorrel's door closed, that is, a steady restraint on the outside rein, I never thought. The tug and give. That some doors must be closed for others to appear in view at all. That the neck must bow, the body bend to grow supple. If they didn't enjoy it they wouldn't win, said Sorrel's friend, watching his flickering million dollar video stallions skipping sideways in a German sawdust, where we perched under the beams of his mainline mother-in-law's centennial farmhouse. Then we drove on to the ocean. Then she closed that door, about three p.m. with many hours to go. A piece of my brain grew slack and fell to flapping loose behind one eye. Lean over me, read me that part again, so fast spit flies. A slack rein confuses, don't let me see a loop. You want your hands to hold a steady slight restraint and squeeze forward with your pelvis, where everything that counts begins and ends. With the sun setting on her russet flank, that has such heat inside it.

Now I take in every word. I keep the menace cycling. Writing wrecked us, you are saying, we were strong before the printed word. It was type branded us witches. Type helped burn nine million at the stake. But who invented the alphabet? I see a parallel inkless fate. Me in a circle of relatives around a stingy fire hearing the same continuous dusty tale. Some desperate daughter scratches on papyrus, frees us from the endless family fable. The one with tattered

fur counting her coffee beans and buttoning her cuffs or
falling in love, unregenerate, with an old fox, she invented
writing. Trapped, she will speak into bars of soap or into the
air, nothing stops her, or on the wall of the prison with
excrement. But that wasn't your point, I know. You meant
what do you grieve? I take in every word only to dispute it.
Then I give them lodging. What I read on the walls are
centuries of resistance. A subterranean menace. I simply
want your chestnut grasslike fur to go forever. Stones,
witnesses, implacable as photographs, slightly malevolent.
Your bitterness and the formal beauty that disputes it. Are
we starving mustangs? Your sorrowful face and the heat
you press on me that belies it. You simply wanted to be able
to say yes, no, at random.

Down by the canal behind the laundromat among bottles
condoms you can see a cinnamon dove. Why they invented
angels. To explain this heart hunger fed by the eyes starved
by the world. One black rubber flipper floats on the mild
brown waves, signifying a rise or renewal after defeat.
Behind the laundromat by the dirty water one sat down and
said where could he learn English. He worked above the
lake at the chicken farm. He chooses them, you see, one goes
here the rest there. And it breaks him, it is very sad, you see,
he says, because their sexes, you know, is like ours.

Like ours? But they save the ones that lay eggs, right? Is he
saying, you and me, we aren't egg-layers, we'd be thrown
on the heap? A man parting the legs of thousands of infant
chickens, finds himself far from home, weeping above an
icy foreign lake. They are good at that. (Men, exile, weeping.) Well, I think, pasting a fanaloka over a partial account
of a man bitten 78 times by a rare pit viper, it's not as if the
egg-layers enjoy an enviable fate.

He says it is the beauty of the view that makes the sexing
hurt his heart more worse. And the sexing makes him sad
also thinking of his wife. In the dryer his clothes are seven
shades of natural soil from chocolate mud to salmon sand.

Cincinnati is built on seven hills, rolling red brick, called the
city of seven sisters. The ibis had flown for California with
a Rodrigo by the time I started recording. This accounts for
the shocked freakish nature of the record. Buoyant cereal
three times a day. Spider the size of a baseball mitt. Moans
below when he hit her, pregnant. Walls painted black with
neon pink woodwork. Whole hogs roasting in the sun on
the sidewalk down steep Vine, every possible southern
green thing wilting rotting all the way to Fountain Square.
Nineteen, so full of the vole. Before he left, he and his
mescaline said, "you're all the same color!" We'd dyed our
clothes rust and rose on the stove. Now I was all of them.
After he left, the Delta Queen rocking on the olive green
Ohio, hurt. His first letter back said, "I got clap from the boy
on the corner who sells The Eye." I had to dim out, tangled
in the yetziratic sheets, loosed only by dark night strolls
when it could push out of the chest cavity and fill the sky.
Who could hope to give that a home anyway? Untameable,
briatic. As for colors, ha, mere diversity, I was now all of
them, that's where I would live. I devoured them like a do-
gooder. I believed in the properties of colors, in objects
passing unhurt through panes of glass (unlike Nan, age 22,
drunk and full of voices, falling on a field of abalone shards,
broken buttons). I believed in pens writing with no visible
means of support.

I glue a spitting bobcat next to Bernadette Devlin facing it
with a glistening snarl. Their pale lashes, lash to lash. Both

at home in Arkansas or Belfast. I hit a morass, a drought, a
blank. Begin to have to see a window up close in a vending
machine, too close, full of hard sweet stale things in shit
brown wrappers with letters the color of infected cuts.
Hunger, as a word, empties dry and blows away. Everyone
who loves is standing in a railway station.

A lot of wood polished by wandering sleeves gives it a
sorrel sheen, the rest of the light blue from high dusty
windows along a vaulted ceiling. Sorrel, who has nothing
of this color about her, nothing western, midwestern, no big
warm animals heating the night, gets a Mars bar out of the
machine in the Wilmington train station. For the solitary
return. Plashes fall on it, tears darken the wrapper, the lap.
For the coming ordeal. The train that will catch on fire.
Neither knows this now, we are focused on the present
ordeal. How like heartbreak is bruised pride. The train will
fill with smoke, people will scramble, make high urgent
cries in the dark, get open a window, flail into the black
tunnel, led by a cigarette lighter find a ledge. She will say "I
stayed in my seat. I didn't really care. I only wished I had a
light to read by while I waited." I will say, how can we tear
at something so mortal?

This remembering is making me crazy. For times like this I
carry lead letters on tiny wooden blocks, 9 point, *l*, *d*, *g*, *w*,
garamond italic. Their sharp serifs, the vestiges of ink deep
in their clefts. Put *d* next to *g*. Once I argued with someone.
Put a *w* between them. Don't think these are people, these
are the chords that link you to the unobstructed universe.
The doors close behind me. *D*. This is my letter. Door. This
is for me. This is not an ending, but the doors are closing
behind her! says a younger voice. Close isn't part of my
name. I'm not looking back and what is ahead. Give me a

little help here, Jesus Christ. Come on. "Come on," she'd say. "Put your arms around me."

Don't interrupt me. I'm seeing two bones through my door. No, two standing stones. Or wrists perpendicular with something quick and white between. Lighting up a dark heavy blue. Hitting the tops of grasses. Brief intermittent messages reaching the throat, middle, and thigh. The on off pressure against a shank. Peace. Called keeping the door closed. As a signal parts the weighted midnight. Months. About two volts. About one third as sharp as grabbing a live wire in the rain trying to open the gate. The heart beats in response to such impulses but don't interrupt to illustrate. Or riding blindfolded which turns the world a rusty chestnut shot with shocks of light. Thinking of uninterrupted static, practicing to hear my mother's voice one day in white noise. She was speaking in words composed of syllables in French and English, alternating, of something tender yet to come. In the meantime, d, g, w, l, can be paperweights to keep the edges of the pictures from ruffling in her passing.

Out on the sidewalk now in this town named for trees, trees are making many voices, are you ready? What a diversity of greens. Spite, like spit, rises fast once you decide to dispute whatever you find, for no good reason. I pocket my slugs.

I cover over a secret place a brackish pond red black still water, with a mule gone white. My other heart commits murder. With more serious self-witness than the man from Florida. The hidden heart (murderer) does the choosing now. I just ask the pictures where they want to go. Give it rein, I say, all art, mockery, and indigence. Caged and furious. Here is another cat, leopard like the muff. A leop-

ard-skin muff with pink silk interior which Sorrel took as a
sign of my intent. I meant as a sign of—oh, the wonder of
objects, a world that kills a leopard to make a muff, horror
made beautiful. I said, "Put your hand in here." "That's
when I knew you were trying to seduce me," she said. The
leopard's hind legs are now on higher ground. Fixed in its
leap by a lake of snotty glue (can't stand to have dry edges
ruffling up) over today's ripped words: "above a niche a
naked man crouched and llet smashes to smithereens the
gallant dancing run with almost desperate force casional
embraces carry small statues when he comes abruptly
breaking their littleheeled slippers more reluctantly to different parts of him roughly turns off the others taunts or
longings."

"I don't desire you anymore the way I want to," Sorrel said,
scaring up birds like sheets, like nuns, floats, birds neither
of us could name. What do I hate? That we moved to a
cheaper, browner, mustier motel just when I needed a shell.
Or that I didn't know the names of the giant birds we
startled up from the swamp. Making the birds scatter. I
don't have to stay here in the barren bird preserve. That's
what fiction's for. I paste a postcard of a blue-black panther
from Busch Gardens across the words "barring journalists
from entering," saving another defunct angel, summoning
another dark-haired woman's name, two soothing syllables, no hiss.

I paste a picture of a shy chocolate fanaloka over an account of murder from the Ann Arbor News. "A woman was arrested in Toronto for attacking a man with a cordless drill." The remote fanaloka (fossa fossa) is Mary, thus I make balance.

Mary was a model waitress. Her short black hair on a long white neck, a French neck, a cinema neck. It was a cinema town. I am twenty-one. Mary wipes down her tables at 3 a.m. She dunks her whole head in the sink, a palmful of gardenia shampoo, a good catholic girl on whose marble body no amount of depravity dare leave a mark. Glistening, she makes me a Pimm's cup to buoy me up as I scrape the grill with the block, steaming my face with the smell that dogs always follow, after I leave her. Mary took the fall for all the friends who brought Flaming Creatures to the screen and were arrested for obscenity. On the stand, what man could send the Virgin Mary to jail? He could do worse. One of her jurors. Terrible hair low on the forehead, followed her to our bar. This will never have happened, because of the panther I have placed between them. Along the margin of a ripped piece of the Ann Arbor News the words: "touched by her testimony." touched. "She likes to have her face touched," Mary announced one night after closing. To my

invisible future comers. She didn't like me to use big words
like closure, synchronicity. Am I pasting for Mary? No, I
make balance. I make everything up.

Mary had been writing her memoirs by tossing scraps of
paper into a box. Some original notes, some things overheard.
Names of Motown groups she was inventing. Pictures of
herself naked in the rafters in karate postures. As long as she
was in the body cast, she was a lesbian. Only a finger could
enter her. Men at dawn on the porch photographed her bike
after removing the light. She lost the suit against the man
who hit her. When I came home from the bar she'd say, "I
creamed myself in my cast, give me a kiss." There was an
Alaya, how to spell it, that she had loved. If I could find Aleia
now I could write Mary's memoirs because at least half that
boxful was mine or Eliya's. And we'd call it My Own Story
by Teeny Chiffon.

A lesbian is a memoir. Anything a lesbian writes arranges
or steals and pastes is read as autobiography, pathology,
already sexed and traceable. Mine will be more like a train.

Two years before, in the bathroom mirror in Athens, Ohio,
I had seen every one of my years to come, nineteen to ninety,
speeding by blue and red in veins suddenly visible beneath
transparent skin stretched tight with astonishment at so
much momentum, exactly how it would look: frowning,
fierce, adamant about the body's right and every woman's
body's right to be inhabited and to press them together. The
word that rose then was not 'right' but vehicle. Then the
bathroom door opened to screams, I forgot everything for
years. An ice white ibis had been hit in the mouth, his tooth
fell in his palm, his palm filled with blood. I drove, steering
from as far away as Venus, to the emergency room where

I refused to give the name of my gay comrade, Clay, my best friend, son of the man who owned the bowling alley where the football team beat us up, first lover, gay soon after. The doctor and nurses joking about pizza, don't you think these girls would like some pizza, because they knew drugs turned our hungry minds to mouths and only girls have mouths. That will go in one compartment.

Trimming around the meager tail of a zebra cut from the National Geographic, I remember National Velvet's paper horses. Don't mistake repetition for balance, I tell myself firmly, pressing two emerald snakes emerging from its mouth and anus. I paste a story (what's a story?) of a pioneer boy consumed by a tapeworm set to die by a bowl of water just out of reach until thirsty enough out it crawls. So much for elementary education. Do they have eyes? Do they have mouths? Can snakes be bandaged? That's all I had to know. Then I could be their angel. What I saw in a mirror in Athens, Ohio—two girls with hair in braids wound around naked breasts, a woman wrapped in foil, gay boy dancers making sharper angles, masturbating, one bleeding from the mouth—that was reflected behind me. What I saw in my face, my future, Polaroid speed, prophetic, I'd say about 70% accurate, that was just veins. I was always reading into things. I paste a Bazooka gum fortune across the back of an Appaloosa like a soft Sioux Indian saddle; it says "Angels guard your every step." Under its hoof I write chain lightning. Is the wild water out there too beautiful? Does it distract you in your furious efforts to understand?

I take a smoking stance against the wall beside the green water with its fawn-colored foam. I gave up smoking after the accident because lighting up drew eyes to the bent limb. What happened in Ireland was when I was trying once and for all really trying this time to be a man, knocked down and the green twig fracture grew greener bluer yellow sky before a tornado. You are trying so hard not to be a man you go numb. Dead Man I write on your forehead where you stare from your waking sleep.

Mary and I had planned to sleep in the middle of Avebury Circle. "Where is your protection?" said a boy, a waiter at the pub. We laughed. "You! you are our protection. Aren't you a man?" "Brain pudding," he said savagely. All night long lying among the stones we heard whistling in ever narrowing circles, accompanied by lowing querulous cows sounding as if they knew the normal course of dusk, deep night, dew, had been disturbed at the core of the world. Nuts fell on us like bullets. We were safe as anyone home in the family bed. The great stones grew pink, and still we couldn't read the words.

I said "water" to Mary when she fell and knocked her head. In her stupor she dreamed I said it, demanded water, water. Now we both believe in it for concussion, for anything, communicating with the dead, the might have been, the far away, for discommunicating, purging, all that. When someone feeds your love to the river. Mary, are you listening? Water. We broke the ice on Lake Michigan, stripped and jumped. Down jackets waiting on the shore in two puffs, one blue one rust. There was another swim in the dark at a Camp Covert. I looked back to see her on shore, two great man shapes alongside, swam furiously to be her protection. They pointed to a beached and twisted boat. "That got caught in the undertow you just swam through," they said, revealing badges. I can say and Mary was my witness, that I swam through the undertow and out again. But I don't know if I would have had she not been standing whitely on the shore. We have the double exposure during a photo session in Saginaw Woods, me clutching a bundle of rags, white paint on my face, her with branches in her hair and camera in front of her face. It was a charm for disappearing and truly the edges of Mary are beginning to blur. But when the edges disappear, the substance can really travel. No, this accident was later, near Duncannon, Ireland, a little interior snap. It won't appear here.

A memoir can be made the same way. Take any novel and pretend its autobiographical. Take some things out, put some things in. A lesbian is a woman who reads without respecting anything. Where is the authority in these words? A lesbian or a memoir neither has nor answers to authority. A lesbian is a memoir in the eyes of the world. Someone can make you a lesbian by saying "I thought so because of the way your mouth turns down when you smile."

"Who wants to read about all the women she was with?" your mother asked you. Answer, "I have been with 2,283 women." Two squirrels girdling a tree in a day and a half felled 2,283 twigs to get at seeds. The tree with all its pendant spheres is starting to topple because of all the women I have girdled and trimmed. Two thousand two hundred and eighty-three women. Think about it. You're forced to.

In a Chinese restaurant in San Francisco and I asked Mary how many she said, "Oh not many, 50." I said I thought 22 was too many. She said, "Well Clay lost count at 4,000, so why do you feel sin? We were pioneers." Her fortune said, 'your lover will never want to leave you.' Mine was a blank white strip. A moment came back to me. A passage in Delta of Venus read standing up in Borders Bookstore. The bathroom in Jacobson's across the street to get off. In the stall

next a woman in high heels facing the toilet like a man.
Sound of pissing. What is a lesbian, I was still asking myself
at twenty. So I asked the heels, "Can you tell me what a
lesbian is?" He passed me a tube of lipstick called walnut
and I knew that meant Hester Prynne, a lesbian is a prostitute, because Hester stained her lips with walnut juice.
English majors run to their texts. Nothing. See, to a memoir,
literature is not sacred. I read it, it became mine, it lay with
the others and merged as memoirs are wont. Who can say.
Who can say what? Who can say what a lesbian is. A
memoir is a manifesto is a lesbian fucking literature.

You. Sleep with 2,283 women. Girdle the tree of life below
the snow line and strip it, watch it fall. Sleep with 22 men
and live to tell. Feel as little love as possible, even for the tree
circled with ivy, the one that watched over you that com-
forted and rocked you and said s/he'd never leave you
strangle it at the root.

Memoirs are not romantic. Even when they wallow they
fail. The flat statement at the soul of the memoir is I can't feel.
The lesbian can relate sentimental facts. But to write ro-
mantically the lesbian must be an author this is a contradiction
in terms. No I. A memoir cannot refer to another with any
objectivity. There is no other. A memoir that begins You....

When a memoir reaches out to an ephemeral other, books
fly off the shelves into your arms, A Great Love, State of
Grace, Ravages, Night, Dusty Answer. Led to believe we
stave off the natural rot by loving women carefully, correctly.
I mean, in all their diversity, confusing them with us.
Violent loving, lesbians believe, disintegrates the integrity
of the memoir, writing itself at the kitchen table this very
moment, inserting itself into the underside of history, writ-

ing very close together to kill fewer trees. When a lesbian says love he or she means pride of self. A lesbian is a Hercules. A lesbian really loving women drops the earth, forests fall. Nothing means anymore. Look what happens. Worse you can't tell who. You are. A memoir about really loving is a contradiction in terms, if a memoir is a lesbian. You do this. You make me say these things.

I am writing your memoir I will make you feel, Dead Man. I am in you you are putting down your pen, putting down your coffee. A sharp pain below a rib on the left that's me climbing crossing diagonally. Circling your heart and squeezing. You made me. Wetness on your lashes now, this moment. You are thinking, looking at the steam rising from the lake as from a new corpse, that you have missed the point and maybe it's too late. You don't know what you are. How dare another woman make you feel this way. It's not real. It's only a footnote. Yet you have never been so alone, many times. A pioneer.

She sat up in bed and said, "I don't know how to love. I am a dead man." Dead Man, I wrote on her forehead. I always have pens in the bed. Woke with her cheek in a pool of ink. "Look, my spit is blue," said Sorrel, the echo of her name adding an animal rust to the violet blue. This is a deep green night wood. This is a blue-black panther, my companion. Talk to Bast, bide with Nuit. I put it three-fourths up a waterfall near Machu Pichu, mercury, throat. A warm cave in the throat behind the green fall of water. It speaks with the voice of Maat. Paws crossed, eyes slit in utter objectivity, somnambulant grace, before the fire wherein arise the images. Here is a postcard from Wilmington, a painting of a thin naked woman on the moor, "Doesn't this look like your white snake body? My train caught fire."

In China they say I should have had an egg instead of you. In The Realm of the Senses he puts an egg back inside her. Three women around a bucket floating eggshells in Portree, framing spells. She sat up in bed and said "eggs, eggs" and called me angel. This is a walnut night wood, a fourposter, a thin snaky name scratched out of the varnish. Sorrel. Where are all the wild feelings now? My great aunt Birdie, 101, lay in the bed she was born in, Berea, Kentucky, starving, silent, furious. Having pitched her scrambled eggs against the wall. She just stub up. Mad at the state of things, when a woman can no longer feed herself.

You ain't made no angels, you ain't got no angels says the radio sermon channel voice, set against, rubbing himself against lipstick, midwives, women writing and rubbing themselves. Every town in Ireland once supported a mid- wife and a mourning woman, according to my aunt Birdie. Where are all the wild feelings now? Right where they always were, undiminished, under the sternum.

The mare bulges out at every corner, unrepentant, bending herself like rubber. If I close my eyes it grows as long, this bulge, as the side of a ship slowly rolling over in waves higher and greyer. We are rolling over, something sinks like a ship. And down down, such relief after fighting the waves the curves, miles down no one can expect a struggle, to hang in darkness where another phrase or image might pull you out. You? I've abandoned her to you. Me. I'm talking to her directly, I'm nowhere. I'm the eye watching her sink.

Something pressing to be said. It can't get near enough to speak, or I don't like it. To the left over the left. The sinister hand. It's called 'soft eyes' when you ride without focusing on anything you have eyes all over your head. Your direction is determined by your pelvis, squeezing the two of you forward, no object. So much love takes place at this bend, peristaltic, kundalinial, vision that reaches the brain and disintegrates into patterns of whining, songs on the radio, little jabs in the dark.

Soft eyes. Cool warm wounds, heat cool wounds. Soft hands. Adhesive seat. So you don't interfere with the way she has to distribute her weight to carry you. Something is pressing. The mare her muscles bunched, starting to loosen, shaking her starry mane, pressuring me to the left...coming into me through my side between ribs a nightmare snake the kind of thing that can enter through skin when it needs to speak. But not yet able to hear it.

I didn't mean to do it. Was it coldblooded? "I thought it was a little coldblooded," Sorrel said. "I really loved what you did but I thought it was a little coldblooded." At the sink she says the fleas crawl out to the eyes to save themselves. You have to cover her eyes with Vaseline and her genitals. "Come help me. It makes her so cold. She's like a newborn kitten again when she's soaked. Wrap the towel." There will be no time to debate what I did, I thought, because of the morning's escape. But here it is evening of the same day, car dead, night again, and ready, a ready easy lie. A good warm shape to it, I say, "No not cold. I wanted to say goodbye. I wanted to give you something." Of course it was coldblooded it was bloodless it was a little knife of ice. It was an icicle, fucking her with an icicle. And I got a lot out of it, I did. I got what I wanted. Some small shiver of revenge, some measure of mine, back, silent and mean. Even at my meanest you see it can pass for generosity. All the more satisfying.

So how go on after such a natural ending? So accustomed to finality, fatality I meant fatalism. Nothing is ever lost I keep repeating, something in me frozen long ago on the word. Of love. And of cruelty? That too grows tangled and enmeshed so I am back, it's still September, we're still here with the bed, and somewhere in the bed is the thing I left, how I thought I was above this stinginess of spirit. So to punish myself, no, to acknowledge myself I let her try.

I guess it has three parts. The third part has four minutes and belongs to the future. The phone will ring, nothing is ever over by default. To get even or to get it back, or to fill the space. The third part takes place in the space of the dream I dreamed after I let her try: there is a war. women are standing too far apart. Unless they take this seriously, they will die without being able to help each other over. They will die alone. I have to take out the em space and replace it with an en space between all of them so they can reach each other. "Don't laugh, pay attention," I say out loud in my sleep, "there's too much space." "I'm Barbara Bush," she says from somewhere in the bed.

Moon blacked out in the sky. Hinged piece of time. Fixed. In a dim kitchen sound of frogs first on the left then on the right the sides of the brain calling to each other. Her eyes back and forth so fast on my face meaning please don't go. Mine held. Seized up. Staring to whiteness. A fixed dismay. Then a stick chewed in the middle is being chewed and is apart white sudden space opens and freezes. Call it implosion. Or some kind of seven of swords, losing at the moment of grasping, as if the strength were exhausted. As if? Cyclical as the progression women's bodies know— innocence, then fear, its focusing, its terrible despair, the knowing without the acceptance, the blood, then the acceptance, the vision again, hunches working, helping, then the buildup, the seizure, the fear, the terrible blind despair, the thing surfacing, forced into view, the fixed dismay. Necessary to separate, to bleed, so as to see. Necessary to see to come together ever again in another. Things stop. Protection is lifted. Change breaks to shape.

Chinese letterpress needs 5,000 lead slugs. Don't know the exact figure. On the sidewalk, fingering the English letters, remembering China. The first sign: a couple, an Asian woman and a blond man, his face red all over the lower half in a rash. The lower half. I picture him eating her out. Shamefaced, slobbering. Her coming and coming, making sounds without consonants sharp as squawking unknown birds or martial arts. And him sucking blind like a blond infant. Both infants, holding hands in a preverbal wormlike pairing. Preverbal. The Asian woman is learning English. Idiot sex needs no common language, neither does love neither does hate. All the important things go on without description, mindless primitive driven.

Learning means he is her teacher. That is his job. Of course he is taller. She is dumb, speechless, cunning, attaching herself to someone taller, whiter, richer, more articulate, teacher. Words become deteriorated.

This couple on the walk, when they fuck, is her coming overwhelming? No because it is contained in foreignness, the ultimate feminine, safely speechless. He is teaching her. She is not teaching him. She would have to teach him about double speechlessness, being female, immigrant; triple, being three times other, colonized, unmarried, speechless

female. What comes out of her, when she comes? That
burns his face so? Caustic vowels, vengeance in the shape
of acquiescence, little girl, mother, student, silenced? In his
debt. Does it burn his tongue? But does it burn his tongue
enough? 5,000 characters with which to keep secrets, funnelled
into a few crude English phrases: I love you. Thank you.
Stay with me. Do that more.

The second sign: the Asian woman in the shower with the
body of my sister's child, who named herself Napoleon,
round in the belly, flat chested, protruding buttocks, is
washing endlessly. A healthy 28-year-old 12-year-old. Next
to her I am ancient, dusty, reptilian, whiplike clearly her
other half, her assassin. Continents open between us and go
to war. My body has been shaped to flail her false innocence
my false privilege into bloody froth. Napoleon—

or Nap, as we called her, not knowing I was listening, was
speaking Greek to her Greek grandmother, teaching the old
woman English. Yaya sits tatting, smiling encouragement
from the big smug continent of age. "Yaya," says Nap,
"Here is how you say I love you in English: I puke on you.
And here is how you say thank you: fuck you. And here is
how you say: you are welcome, repeat after me: you are an
old man's fart." What was Yaya's crime besides binding the
baby's limbs in the crib? A cellular cruelty bled into the
lining of the uterus? Toxic, absorbed from all sides? Can we
pass laws against poison jealousy? Words become corroded.
I am most qualified to speak.

What had made him say, "How could you open your legs
to all those people?" Oh, his own limbs had been bound and
otherwise subjected. Poor child. And his rich white father
before him, we can be sure. What made her go back to him?
I see her legs opening, taking him in, where he is joined by
an alphabet of little dancing men, 5,000 characters, 5,000

possible combinations that she, in her superior ancient cunning, lies so shamelessly in front of the camera, will never reveal. Never reveal me. Never give the satisfaction. Never return. Signs to recombine in love and hatred, while that mouth, her two mouths colluding, that dissembler, says "down" all drawn out in that loose oval way. They have.

From her white china throat. The presents she gave me from April on: a photograph of an ice cube melting on a piece of white bread seeming to be suspended in the black universe. Another of a can of spaghetti, the p a h removed, sgetti and of tomatoes, the t o removed matoes. sgetti matoes. That was the third sign: we were in a diner in upstate—means mountainous places full of straw people, the kind with straw hair straw eyelashes pale straw eyes—and two were drunk one making fun of the other. "Tell them what you eating, guy." "Sketty matas." A pale green jade bracelet from China. A box with a postcard of Chillicothe (for my straw kin, my lash-lessness) one white and one black horse glued to the floor and a moon swinging from the ceiling for Stephen Foster. Reams of stationery from hotels all over China. "Look," sitting on her paisley couch drinking sherry, "is it fair?" she asked referring to her position, or her married status, which did she mean? And mine, unmarried and floating through the work world. Completely opaque to me, this question of position. I was free, a free agent. She seemed a being buried alive, buried in an airless room so stifled she fell asleep on her pages every day at three. In a house she didn't like in a rural town she hated too many rooms all full of old furniture full of postcards, a hoarder. Did she mean was it fair that she hung on to everything especially things she no longer wanted and I let go of especially what I did? "Things don't match," she said in my car, car's front foot on a rut of mud. I was in

it, that bruised ground, forever sunken, a once riotous
element, hardening white. She is remembered innocently
to me by others as a wild Chinese-American schoolgirl in an
all dyke bike gang. All of her sisters and brothers get
together each year and discuss how much the parents
ruined. The whole family went to China, seeking the house
where the parents fell in love. Back home she married him.
Left the house in the square. Then she left the husband.
Never return, she said.

But her hands. Should have been a warning. Powerful
little hands. Short fingers always curled and somehow
grasping. Curve around food like a raccoon. Don't offer
themselves, straight, long, graceful, to love to feeling the
world of skin like eyes. Don't offer. Curled and very
short. The shortness, stunted almost. My fingers are long
and they let go. My cousin's hands held the bowl in the
Betty Crocker ads. All powerful hands in this family, can
rein in a horse, can work a seizure out of a tendon...it was
that curve. Like a paw. The curve of a kind of dream,
greedy, desperate, and she is disappearing, the mother,
you would kill to keep her from going out that door. And
another thing, her hands were always cold; the thing
they curved to hold was cut off at the root, no blood
flowed. Think of those hands, rehearse that curve, now
do you want those hands on you? You can always find a
vault in the other's body vivid with shape and horrible
color to hold back your cries, the ones you don't want
opened again, pried open.

Her mother passed along a hatred of whites so intense for
years her daughter believed they smelled of spoiled cottage
cheese. Her mother told her, in line at the grocer, her voice
become a great sorrow, look at them. They have no bones,
they whine, snap, crumble at the slightest disappointment.
Their young are puffed up like blisters and their old are bent

double from supplication. They don't wash, they wear their dead skin cells like moldy furs. Their blotchy pinkish skin like pigs pig-colored and their pale lying eyes behind lashes like straw. Straw people, slow to evolve, pigsty people.

A Chinese Maat saying, "I make balance," breaking straw people in both fists, hollow reeds raining on the earth without seeds. Her daughter married and left a redhaired man. Debauchery and its attendant pleasures. The mother and daughter fight in the hotels from which she sends me stationery in many colors, each tiny character letterpressed by hand. They would have fought anyway. Her daughter would have gone back to him anyway. Her daughter doing that with a white straw woman, not so much the *that*, as the void opening under her eldest, now stained, unmarriageable, become other. "We compromised," she said. "I agreed to let you go, and mother agreed not to kill me."

"She broke her promise," I said.

Moved by silenced riotous elements. Or a color in a Fury comic book, blue-black ink that seeped into me and lay in wait for her china hair, heavier than anything on this continent, against her blue-white throat that came on the boat from China. Things don't match. So that you can see yourself standing out, standing against, throwing against, so that you can see yourself in relief, in motion, so that you can feel your draw, your convulsion, your cells a honeycomb, permeable, running, irresistible, so you can feel that the current doesn't circulate inside, silkworms digesting shitting dying, but leaps across into another, darker it is, the brighter the egress, lighting her eyes, making her eyes water, making her eyes hard as she defines herself in opposition, leaving you, but leaving you changed.

Before white terror comes after. They ask me what comes

next. Blood bath. How can I tell them we have to give our
bodies? They will do it. But they are children. I can't do this
anymore. Her face grey-white just exactly like Diana
Oughton's face. Bernadette Devlin's. Mairead Farrell.
Women in jail denied even buckets write Free Ireland on the
wall with fingers in shit. Never forget. Have seen too much.
Of course it is possible to see too much. To watch unroll,
Cassandra, all your power fully, finally, and watch it fail to
save a hair on a head. Even to wonder if your seeing didn't
send them to their graves. Once they saw it your way.
Conviction feeds conviction. To know it will all be for
nothing. Or for some game in another body, hardly a notion
to give you peace, even if you believed it.

Deep hidden tributary of hate who would ever own, running into wide Mississippi of jealousy. Moved by this bile
rising or by exhausted faces of heroic strangers. Always the
distance of literature. Or the distance of obsession. The ones
who elect one, going on a common conviction brotherhood?
feminism? more or less in love with loving widely. Who is
most qualified to speak. When you begin to love, you can
see, you think, straight into a soul like your own, in a body
and history so different, jeweled, mesmerizing. Where does
it turn. Or when you are fired by the words of such a one to
go outside yourself for others, for a future you believe you
can shape. This too can leave you if your lover leaves you.
Flat, unable to watch the news. Walk past an occasional
headline. Swept up in a great striving. How many have to,
you know, die to teach you simple commonplace compassion. How to pull someone out of harm's way by
seconds. Or, your lover leaving you can move you closer to
it, the suffering you shut out against your pleasure. Away,
that is, from paralysis, a small lift toward any living weeping thing, old man in overalls bent over a slip of paper in the
bank, loud, into silence.

But I am still alive. I think I am the most qualified to speak. It is also my obligation to inform everybody. The first sign: police car crashed into four innocent people. Second sign was some soldiers abandoned their arms, gave uniforms and equipment to people and students. The third sign was shown on June 3, 2:10 p.m. A large number of army loudspeakers said "people's police love students" as they stabbed in the abdomen. Soldier said "who loves you" and stabbed. Situation became deteriorated. Students in square stood up with right hand, "We swear we will... protect...citizens from...white terror"...even until I am the last.

Emergency messages received from all sides. Fired on everyone who shouted or even held a brick. Bleeding in the chest. Blood on hands, chest, legs. Last drop of blood of the comrades hugged together in anger. From April onward.

Highest purpose of peace was sacrifice...hand in hand we went slowly...north west south international. We sat quietly without calm gaze we were involving in a battle of love and hatred not a battle of violence and army force. Our voice would become a great sorrow. Petroleum and bottles assault rifles tanks every one of us standing firm. They went out to negotiate and make compromise of the army. We compromised that if we left. We left peacefully executioners broke their promise.

Reached the third stratum before. Fired like a honeycomb. People around us said "lets stop sweeping" we'll return. We realized only after that some in square still have hope. They thought the troops would try to remove. Tanks crushed them like minced meat. More than 200. 1,000. Don't know the exact figure. Troops poured gasoline over the camps, clothes, corpses. Washed the ground with long-handled brushes to remove bloodstains.

Later we received reports. Fired houses on either side children and aged hadn't even shouted a slogan. I think I am the most qualified to speak. Put our hands on your chests. Can you say they are riotous elements? If they were, will they just sit there quietly? What should we call those who lie so shamelessly in front of the camera? Words become deteriorated. A truck rushed toward us and fired rolled over legs and necks. Many no longer had a complete corpse. Who are the riotous elements? We are alive yet there are many others who left in the square will never return. Very young. Never return. Military vehicles drive full speed. Darker it is, nearer the birth convulsion.

Something in the stomach mourns the necessity of birth. Of shape. The new little bit of flesh, sticking up like a target. Not all women move to protect their stomachs. A woman was found on Aurora Street at dawn, carrying the baby she had delivered herself of by self-imposed Cesarean, having then stitched herself back up. It is easy to assume another's violent story. It is easy to detach. It is very hard to remember what you have not experienced, because you were absent, you were lying then, or you are lying now.

A woman is found on Aurora Street outside the parking structure at dawn, carrying a blue baby she has delivered herself with a penknife. Blue-green embroidery thread crisscrosses her there and there.

In the hospital she walks, runs, climbs, she is impervious to sedation. We are all here to keep moving. Under the anesthetic she sees shelves for things stored in the stomach. There's a crack and it's a folding bed that folds up with a person in it and the person is just gone. She thinks, single women disappear when they reach this age.
Who chose collapse and why? Her head rises and falls to the far side of this question. Her head moves into the wrong place. She moves to lapse the past, but it's like a vine. The

vine wraps around her wrist, her ankle, and goes straight
up to Neptune. She pulls it out of her vein. Confusion about
whose body—the hands don't match. How horrible, she
thinks, looking down, now I am this man and I can't trust
parts of my own body. They are making her string red and
green speckled french horticultural beans. She pulls the
stitches out of the rows. To one side she sees teal blue roses
on a dark bush. It's night. She thinks they came from Jupiter.
She will ask her grandmother how to paint night. She hears
herself speaking as a child, she remembers her name, Nan;
she is slipping out into narratives. "It was like a storage
place I was in. There was a body, and then, on the way out,
I was the one holding the knife, so I must have made the
cut." Was it lost or was it stolen?

She pieces Latvia together. Her favorite movie goes boating.
Sometimes they say they left to look for her mother's
brother, sometimes they say to escape. Celine and Julie go
boating again. Her mother swollen with fifty years. Exits
saying Czechoslovakia. The daughter takes a pill. Their
children become their hunters. All her young life
unblemished by war. She asks, he answers army, sometimes,
sometimes police. They say sometimes France, prison,
Siberia. Unblemished except for a bottle of aspirin at age
fourteen and a large piece of a kidney. No one knows what
happened in Czechoslovakia, her mother says, exiting.
What, she says what? This is the first time for Czechoslovakia. Up to now everything didn't happen in Latvia, where
no promise holds. No one knows, her mother says, unable
to tell. Everything is breaking loose. Her heart holding fifty
years not for this glastnost, not for her, or her brother,
vanished, returned but dead, but dead and still walking.
From where? Depends which year you ask. Everybody
feels so sorry for the Jews, she says, disappearing through

the doorframe with her sewing. She only speaks in passageways or as she sews. Her daughter is used to a trail of words with no face, flung over a shoulder, framed in walnut wood or muffled, accompanied by humming. She brings home talkative New York Jews. Surrounds herself with them. The silence around a word creating a compelling void, a lifelong pull. The Baltic camps rise suddenly out of fog in 1975. Ten years later the grandson has to do a family history. My brother served in three armies, Latvian, German, Soviet, her father tells his grandson. You can always ask me anything. You don't know what was happening in Czechoslovakia, her mother tells her. *What* brother? she asks her father, astonishment as familiar now as a menstrual cramp. Another country never uttered is resurrected and banished in the same month in the same year. You can't stay home from school just because you've started having periods, her mother tells her, the habit of silence too strong to resist. Another daughter is disappeared. She takes a pill and reconstructs the lives of servant girls. She takes blue pills in sequence or at random for the periods.

We have not invaded each other's personalities. We are neither of us raw material. This is about our constant mystery. We are at pains to disguise the splinter under the layers of fictions. She rests her head in the zone of forgetting, where contradictory impulses cross producing sparks and shorting out the system. We have cultivated a boundary between old and new, though it is a mobile one. More than a screen or a wall, it has volume, and tends to be circular, like an innertube. This boundary conceals the places where lines cross, by encircling those felt to defy continuity. It harbors the arbitrary, the hypocritical, the ill-considered, the neglected.

In truth, quite a few things were not lost or stolen, but simply thrown away. As a child, she wanted to be taken seriously, such a hopeless prospect. Any clumsy move she made, when mocked, was never again attempted. Until she had withdrawn to the point where only danger could move her to action. So she cultivated danger as a spur. Sufficient danger to warrant seeking and denying, experiencing and becoming numb. Even as her body was a prison, it was maintained as a pagan shrine. It took extremes to reach her.

She is thinking of her high school boyfriend, Tony. Under anesthetic, some things resurface with a will, like the piece of green glass that disappeared inside Tony's foot in 1969 and suddenly reappeared in 1973, still green, but now surrounded with a rusty halo, a tiny kayak approaching the surface of the sole, begging her to be the one to cut it out. Like her, it was a foreign object, traveling blindly toward the light on the other side of the skin.

I tell her: scale the night. Open an old place. Pull and find where it is attached. Trace it to the foundation (this word may mean moon or genitals). Don't counter it as before, as I did. Memory drives the train.

Things she buried are bound in dreams and words. The place where that hidden by a shell of indifference can be passed through like a comb. Long ago she dreamed of a long white hall with a low ceiling, ending in a room with blue tile and a clawfoot tub. All along the walls of the hall were built-in drawers holding the brides and grooms off wedding cakes. All the brides look shocked, caught dreaming on the way to the guillotine. But when she found this room, in Cincinnati, she had to have it; she had dreamed it. She left home, moved in with Tony. She took care of him.

He'd had it removed from his foot, he was on crutches. Camilla Hall and her cat had just been burnt to death in San Francisco. Tony hated these rooms, their cramped dimensions, the stove named Dixie Wanderer. They lived there anyway, for awhile, sleeping on a pile of blankets. He and his crutches made forays into the night.

Now Nan wakes in a hospital above the Ohio river, by an abandoned button factory. Outside the grid of her window, the ground is littered with abalone. She finds herself engaged. To an intern at the psych unit where she lately makes her home. She is remembering, with ardor, the buttons on Tony's jacket, slate grey, and the way his voice broke in wonder, his hair fell forward only for her. Was his one of the voices inside saying yes or outside saying no? What does she remember of the recent event—the void or the voices inside? Who can remember pain like that, you can't even remember it as it is happening. You are busy in a more compelling country. Later people act astonished at the gaps in your account, as if you are being lazy or stubborn, as if you couldn't remember 9 x 9.

They are afraid. You could be staring at them now and forgetting his face, her particular lovemaking. You could be your own separate creature in a body that had desires it can't remember for people it can't name. They want you to remember and they want you to forget.

They want me to forget my longing for Nan. How when Tony left for the coast with Rodrigo she would sit on my floor and rock and pretend to be cradling a gun. When she went to bed, she would wad a bunch of nightgown between her knees and rub them back and forth with a shsh shsh sound. I loved her. I lived inside my head. I was the one who was watching.

The woman found on Aurora has lived through everything her intern/fiancé has hidden from. He is hypnotized. He wants her to say, "I am not now who I was then. The pleasure you missed was really a lie. The scars I have are my punishment, whereas your scars were all inflicted from outside by an unjust world, by women like me—selfish, amoral." He frequently pictures her in attitudes of remorse, entreaty, her thin white wrists held together and extended toward him across the bed.

Instead, Nan says, "I ate crackers and olives. I made a sandwich for a snake. I smoked opium once a year, on my birthday, and kept it in a green velvet pouch with my grandmother's moonstone. That's all I remember of love."

You are always busy forgetting and remembering wrong. The blanks stand out only when they come under scrutiny. Say you are on trial. To suspend in liquid, in space, to suspend jealousy. Say you are held to account. Suspended in mud, the bog people bore the evidence of their violent ends until they were excavated, every fiber of her dress intact, of the rope around her neck, clay red. It was clearly a crime of jealousy, clearly the victim was guilty. To suspend judgment. A truce with memory, perpetually threatening to fall.

They are arguing. Because she opposed him, he calls her a whore. She says, "What is my life if everything I do I have to put behind me? Why do you take my memories and make them into moral tales?" "Because you remember things wrong," he says. "The way you are seen is the way you are, and I am the only one who is looking. And besides, look at what you have done to yourself." In spite of astonishing blanks, she asserts that everything she did was part of a radical guiding principle. She has plenty of reasons for everything. She is looking for a reason she can undo.

She was supposed to take the medication every day, but her intern/fiancé thought it was bad for his child, the child she carried, so she threw it away. Without it, nothing bound her to the hard bed of reason—one voice, male, speaking at a time. Without it many voices spoke at once, from within her, all crying to be set free. She cut out the growing contradiction.

Nan has no memory of the operation she performed. She only remembers the voices, a crowd of them, telling her they were ready. She thought of the zone of forgetting as a necessary armor, a safeguard against violation. Separate from the part that had to be a human roiling in a hot human sea. This is a reason coming undone.

Under ether, some of the first images to reappear are marked by a fine quality of light. For one, she found the Isabella Stewart Gardner Museum. She had been looking for it since she got the postcard from Tony in May of the court with orchids. "How many years ago did we come here? Even though I can't count the number of times I've been back to Boston, it's my first time back to the Gardner. I'd forgotten how beautiful it is. Love, T."

Now there is a blank. Just a place in a woods. A little area, a few feet across, with nothing in it. On either side, all around it, the more alive woods—things stalking things, little purposes…expectation, mystery, death. Is it a path? *Must* it go somewhere? Yes, down into the earth where there are stored...old lampshades. Hateful yellowed lace collars. An antique store on a street in Boston. The light is the cool green of water under ice. She sees herself at nineteen, standing frozen by a tray of tarnished spoons. Tony is combing the boxes for books to resell. She carries a purse from her mother's college days—a long soft tube of pale suede. She puts it down to try on a tweed coat. It vanishes. Beside her a man pushes a stroller and holds his coat together over a bulge at his stomach. She says nothing. She has nothing to suggest, not even the smallest movement. Drawing inevitabilities from chance.

Her birth-control pills were in the purse. They go to a drugstore to get them replaced. How did this work, with no identification? How did the druggist know where she was in the sequence? That must have been the same weekend they went to the Gardner Museum.

While Tony was looking at art, she would have been thinking dark bitter practical things. Who would work so that he could surround himself with beauty? How one steals a purse. Why her mothers fingers move in sleep, keeping the needle in. While he was looking over the balconies into the gardens she was looking at his pale head with fury. Counting the days since she had found him out. Seeing the forty-odd boys and men he had confessed to sleeping with. Counting back two years to seventeen, high school, when she left home and it began—her and him. And them, apparently.

She is locked into place with the burden of his confession by a bond much stronger than love or hate. Sharing his hate for the straight people who hate him, passing by in their expensive clothes, dreaming their simple greedy dreams of marriage, children, townhouse, and at the same time hating his joy in the passing faces, bodies, paintings, music, dance, food. She wants to ruin him, to become him. How to get experience. How to relinquish tenacious habits of caution, passivity, trust.

Is this where we first decided to divide? How to become a blade, with the charming part, the part that wants connection, lobotomized and dangled like bait.

She was in a more compelling country in the Gardner Museum. A single image forms of a cantelope-colored sandstone arch in blue shadows. A cascade of trailing vines and a painting of a woman writing at a desk. It hurts. It was very painful, the woman writing at the desk. Everything the eye lit on was very painful. Women with husbands and fathers, children with mothers. Women who painted and wrote at desks. Windows lit by green lamps in the twilight streets of Boston, where people sat in twos reading hardcover books. Stories in magazines with the words love, daughter, marry. Pictures in magazines of gardens full of iris and lily of the valley. Every evidence of care, false hope, full hearts.

The pills were out of sequence. Soon she was pregnant with Tony's child. Tony had gone to San Francisco with someone named Rodrigo. "You have a cervix like a steel trap," the doctor told her. Removing the slim seaweed cigarette that was to have slowly opened the os. Instead it is squeezed into a tiny waist. She had to be dilated twice.

This was only a little necessary death, the first, but it is a convenient metaphor now, for the intern whose child she has just delivered herself of. Who wishes to establish blame outside himself, somewhere in her past. But where is her past? It was in the train with the money. She blew up the train. Two hot steel doors are pried open like a trap. Inside— a smoky terrain. Many acts of revenge would follow, all taking the form of self-sacrifice. Inside her, nine million women are burnt again at the stake. Everything happens inside her.

Once when I was five I rode through New Orleans in a station wagon and saw one thing: women sipping tea in high pin collars in a store front window. When I was twenty someone asked me while I slept: What do you think of sex? I answered "I'm in a parlor with five-year-old prostitutes. They have no choice, they have to do it." Everything happens inside me.

"Oh grace. I do not know. Why I came to love her so." That's what I heard them singing in my sleep, as I slept through my twenties. I was living on South Division next to the baptist church. Keep a wall of sound between, that is how I listened for anything. An accordion door divided Caroline's room from mine. Once had been one parlor, ugly, but I am making it beautiful now, without changing anything, like opium.

Caroline's half had a fireplace all blocked up, black green tiles, nile tiles, puffs of white plaster in a storm. Mine had a stained glass window prostituting herself to South Division.

No. The window was simply too close to the street. The street had moved in on her. I slept on the floor on an extra

large mattress given me by a boy who believed it was better
to sleep on the floor. While others slept he crept from room
to room, taking albums out of jackets and placing them
round to round to cover the floor and lighting candles in the
middle of each black disk. The point was the silence, no one
woke. When asked he would whisper "Because I have no
formal education." "What do you do in a bed that big?" my
father asked me. Then we fixed the lock. That one time he
drove me back from Ohio, someone had hacked a hole in
my door with a chainsaw. My father used the tools he had
in the current truck. Plants spilled out at us, green ivy trying
to go. My door had a medusa face in the maple whorls. I had
found a button in the street and stuck it on her lip: *Too cool
to fool, UAW*, with a bullet hole in it, now lying in the dust
beside his drill bit. A pact with violence.

Prisms from the glorious window fractured against fern
green walls. I didn't answer to questions. My father, he
never knew how to do with me. He could handle snakes, he
could speak in tongues, he could fix any engine ever made.
I was a greater mystery. He gave me a book of dreams
interpreted. By a man who surely must have dreaded sleep.
Rest here for a minute, have no fear. Only that which can be
transformed is likely to survive.

Parachute curtains the color of my grandmother's southern
skin hung on either side of the magnificent window, lamps
swathed in her color also. Autographed portraits of Katherine Hepburn, Bette Davis, Loretta Young from my mother's
movie star collection. "All the best, Mona, from Myrna
Loy." They wanted us to prosper, the stars, and we, them.
Under the studio portraits I pasted newspaper photos of
stars in disintegration: Jean Seberg before they killed her,
Rita Hayworth getting off the plane when they still thought

it was drink, Vivien Leigh wringing her gloved hands. In the maple wardrobe I kept a buick green 30s suit, an apricot silk blouse, my chestnut embroidered western boots. To dream your boots are envied is a warning to avoid men and boys or meet your ruin.

I'd bought the boots from Molly Bach. Here she is in a photo holding Una. Her hair swags down, she wears what she wore. It was a movie town, everything was documented, we all have stills. Here I am in the embossed chair about to read from Elizabeth's script "blowing a redneck is like eating baloney." Elizabeth is filming the toe of Molly's boot. We weren't to say hillbilly, let alone redneck, when I was coming up. "Hill folk," said my father, "That's what Papa Jim called all us."

Molly sold the boots to get money for court. She had left the Rainbow People's Party but they wanted Una. Una was four. Her name made me see a child with one eye in the middle, something missing. Molly wanted shots for Una, day care, milk without goat hairs floating in it, but the Rainbow House wanted Una. They took Molly to court, got locals to testify that Molly was a junkie, a prostitute, and a lesbian. The judge, a woman, ruled against Molly, saying that a mother might give up the first two addictions for her child's sake, but experts felt rehabilitation in the third case was unlikely. Power to the people. In this way they won the first case for a child's right to be commune property. To dream of downcast children augurs trouble from enemies and seemingly harmless people as well.

One of Molly's other crimes against the people was eating breakfast with me at Mark's Cafe, where I worked the early morning shift. The Rainbow People were supposed to eat together at the long table in their basement, surrounded by mike stands, drumstands, speakers. Groupies cooked rice mush with limp scavenged broccoli. Their group, Speed— a band of blond sixteen year olds—paid the Rainbow Party's bills by playing at frat parties. Their leader John ate in restaurants arranging concerts, gigs, making deals— submarines, reubens, eggs over easy. Free John was their cry when he was busted for dope. Later when he emerged, plump and victorious, pot now a five dollar fine, he began a record company.

Caroline and I never ate at home either. Caroline ate at Frank's Restaurant across from Mark's Cafe. Runny greek yogurt into which she'd stir three pink packs of saccharine. I ate at Mark's in the early dark while I was supposed to be mopping. Strewing the long floor with deep red scented sawdust, languidly sweeping, sometimes just wetting the mop and bucket to leave it looking used. Bagels covered with peanut butter and cheddar cheese. To dream of eating mucous signifies impotence and bottomless grief.

To dream of eggs is a sign of imminent betrayal. To dream of actually eating them reveals that someone seemingly trustworthy will melt into slime. "We ain't carnivores, man," said Una, clumping the stick she carried everywhere since her acid blues festival vision of "Mouths. Mouths, man."

I held the record for flipping them in the air, 22 in a row. We drank our coffee standing up by the light of the big refrigerator. Molly said she dreamed about her mother. "We were driving on the L.A. freeway. Suddenly she began to shrink. I was behind the wheel. I looked over at the passenger seat. My mother had turned into a fried egg." I flipped her eggs in the air. She handed me the chestnut boots, surrendered the child, stubbed out a cigarette on the yellow-stained green glass plate, vanished.

Next door to Mark's Cafe two lesbians named Butch and Star (christened Lou and Pat) ran a shoe repair shop. Butch, the younger, came in early when she knew I was pretending to mop and I made her coffee laced with chocolate milk and cinnamon toast. How did she know I would come to crave it so, seventeen years after? Butch and Star invited Caroline and me to their trailer for screwdrivers. We looked at Star's paint-by-number portraits of dogs. We didn't disillusion them about us, or love. We were in potential. I was moving too fast to catch that lowering ache. They watched over us.

Caroline also painted. Her older sister Marion sat for her. Marion had hair the color of mine, but kinky. With her stick figure and bush of orange hair she looked like a temper tantrum and was in fact frequently enraged. To dream of auburn hair means you will be indicted by the woman you love for shoplifting and frivolity. She read Anna Freud. She had everybody's secret and years of European angst. Caroline often had to choose between us. I modeled for Caroline's art classes at the university. "Where are your underpants," her professor asked me, following us down the hall. Caroline's arms were so weak she couldn't lift a shovelful of sand. The painting hung above the blocked up fireplace—two pink women's bodies one blond one auburn lying together on a mustard shape. No way to prove the redhead was Marion. To dream of seeing a painting of yourself means that people will only offer you masks and love will forever be just out of reach. That wasn't me up there. Nothing happened until after and everything is over now.

We rented our extra room in January to Elizabeth, a photographer who had worked with Leaky. His wife made all the discoveries, she could testify. Elizabeth herself had lived with the Masai and witnessed a clitordectomy. Every morning the soft crinkly sound of saranwrap that she had molded to her body every night, a cure for eczema. During the February thaw Elizabeth and I were sitting on the porch watching bees in the wisteria. "The hysteria is blooming," she said. A blue and white shirt, stunning. In March she said she could not be civil, she was eaten up. I threw my cup at the wall. She said Caroline got the better books, teas, flowers. I shoved her against it. She photographed me against it. Decided to film us in our disarray. In return she gave me the carved balboa nut from Africa, a charm against evil attacks. I hung it above Rita Hayworth in extremis.

I never felt myself to be in any danger. Art watched over us all. Art had lost his voice in the war. 40? 50? don't know what war or prison. Art presided at Mark's Cafe. Down the long black tables Art and I cast our cold eye. 27-year-old chess players cadging free coffee and bragging about the revolution, paranoid about the chemicals in soap, using code names everybody knew, "panther" "whitey." Asking Art where to find the real music in Detroit. Asking me did I know my eyes were san paku. "Drugs," I said. "Refills twenty cents." Art sat silent one long night when I tilted over into opaline oblivion, head on the table where someone had carved Free John. When Art was jailed (for setting up house with his thirteen-year-old niece) Caroline took him cigarettes. He told her, "Lock your fucking windows. The guy who lives above you is bragging about how easy he could slide in he sees something he wants."

Pimps and drug dealers from Detroit moved in on Mark's
Cafe and scared away the customers. The windows filled
with fourteen-year-old hookers. The college boys had a
hard time telling the hookers from the workers, it was the
summer we all wore transparent indian shirts. Several men
in big white hats and white cowboy boots paroled the
entrance and the alley and covered the pay phone. Rumor
had it one, Short Man, had shot his dog and boiled his cat
alive.

I appealed to the women of the Rainbow Party. I had the
idea they could come in force and take up space at the
window tables, discourage cruising, reassure the regulars.
The Rainbow Women seemed to be leaning into feminism
since John had been jailed. Too late for Molly. But John was
freed and they were re-occupied. I started working the
night shift with a woman named Stormy. We got a rifle and
kept it under the counter. Stormy walked me home each
night, with Chomp, a doberman she took everywhere on a
short chain.

Then one day in April, pimps, El Dorados, fourteen-year-
old girls, all were gone. Art was back. Someone told us he'd
borrowed $50 and put a Detroit contract out on Short Man.
College boys and chess players returned and took credit, as
proud of the rifle under the counter as if they could aim and
fire.

Hanging in my window was the nut from Africa. It was
supposed to ward off evil, but then again, Elizabeth had
stolen it. She never felt herself to be in any danger. While we
were under siege at the cafe, she was falling in love with a
singer downtown. In her necklaces (real carved Masai
beads) and clogs and girls' school accent she sat at the Blue

Light Bar each night, the only white. Art tried to tell her she couldn't run in those things. He went with her for awhile, then "Find yourself another colored escort." The night she invited the singer home, his girlfriend appeared with a blade, cut off Elizabeth's buttons and threatened to cut off her head. The boulder, though, came through my window, landing with emerald and amber shards on my large mattress, setting the nut swinging happily. To dream of church windows portends the shattering of your highest aspirations. Your dearest hope will be trampled before your eyes. Henceforth sterile efforts will be your part.

Elizabeth and Caroline left immediately, back to their suburban fields. When the second rock cracked the night, I was alone. I never felt myself to be in danger. I left Elizabeth's nut swinging above the ragged hole. Packed their things into the coal room. Called Elizabeth at her mother's on Lake Shore Drive. Called Caroline at her parents' in Harbor Springs and said I was gone. When would she come back and help me find another? She didn't know when, she was figuring. She figured on giant vanilla pads, furious charcoal funnels, storms of black powder settling on her mother's countertops, palms. Her mother would be screaming, "Caroline, I can't have any mess, I just can't have any mess." I went to the shoe repair and talked Butch into renting me the unit above the shop.

Safe on the second floor, tiny barred windows, miniature sink, counter top refrigerator for bread, apples, wine. Pale beige-tiled antiseptic bath below a green mirror with frosted seahorses. Pale green fold-out couchbed. No doorbell. Bought a new notebook and worked out a plan based on *End of August at the Hotel Ozone.* Cut off my hair with pinking shears. In *Hotel Ozone* the women who survived the third world war are too young to remember before. Have no allegiance. Take whatever they want. Such faces have never been seen, free of all coy, conciliatory, encouraging movements around the eyes, all mouth. Una's prophecy. Dreamed:

Looking at an electric fence—a roll of moving white on which blue globules, tiny planets of liquid, roll together then apart. I am an old man, trying to show twelve young girls how to see electricity. They have to do it, they have no choice. They are all either mad or confused and then they disappear. Pompously I tell them I made them invisible. Moving down the row of stalls I come to a bucket of feed and say, "I can begin to see one of you now; I can see the energy of love in this grain." I go outside. Caroline is smoking a cigarette on a beach. I am furious that she won't swim....I hit her, hard. She falls flat, sticking in the wet sand, then rising, naked, hair in crimped waves, hands clasped to her stomach, Cigarette still dangling from an open mouth, into the sky. Below on the beach next to me is a refrigerator with a crown of antlers. Inside, one half is solid, the other half a moving panorama of field, horses, road. To see a refrigerator in your dreams signifies injury to an innocent friend on account of your greediness. On the other hand, to dream of a reindeer augurs steadfastness to comrades in their tides of woe.

I would wake up every morning to his breathing in the kitchen. The air he breathed he sucked from out of me. To wake up alone, with no one breathing near, is to know the world in all its beauty. The sound of him silenced the songs of the birds, the leaves against the glass, drained each dawn's light of color, made the light dust.

I never meant to replace her. I meant to take over as him, but in my efforts to mimic, practice, imitate action I became hypnotized. Impossible to walk away. Impossible to turn the back.

There are four of us in this dream and we are all guilty. We plotted to kill her, and two of us did. One of us shoved her in the drawer that was supposed to go to the sea, but years later one of our children finds it and pulls it out. We reassemble. One of us points out that our crime has poisoned our lives. Now is our chance to confess, give over the evidence, go to prison, free of guilt. I forgot to say the body of our mother has caved in to a mossy, brown ball of fibers the size of a grapefruit, smelling sweetly of rotten straw and clover. It sits above us on the chiffonier, the chest of drawers that should have opened to the sea. Or, we could get rid of it once and for all. I'm for this, it is now in a very disposable form. But as long as it watches from the vanity, the bureau, the wardrobe, our mother's body, we are marked.

A few years later I see one of us getting into a Grand Marquis. She is wearing some dark fur and emeralds. "So it was right to get rid of the body again?" I ask her. She says, "Yes of course. Now we are all prostitutes under the law."

There are many mounds in Ohio where children, bussed from school for the day, stand and weave and fall, feeling the power through their soles. Fort Ancient is on a high bluff of the eastern shore of the Little Miami—900 acres thickly covered with trees. The serpent's hump rises and blocks the sun, humming. I knew these were the only places where he wouldn't be able to track me, where his thoughts couldn't penetrate the bone of my skull. Mounds, circles of stone, patterns known only from the air. I grew up straining to decipher their hieroglyphics, convinced it was a secret pre-father language, a paradise on earth.

According to Dee Coo Dah, Ohio was once a metropolis of holy circles, private avenues, sacred residentials, heavenly clusters.

Who is this Dee Coo Dah? Once when I was six, I thought I saw her, living in a yellow Chrysler in the Marion Salvage Yard, long black braids, a Hudson Bay blanket made into a coat. She was said to have the Cherokee alphabet. She grew up in Mountainview, Arkansas, where she had copied out the medicine in a little spiral notebook. She healed and cursed, and heated vienna sausages on a kerosene cooker.

He went frequently to the salvage yard, climbing around on gutted cars. The cars in mounds, doors swinging open on leather, cherrywood dashboards, rosaries, garters, naked rubber women hanging from rearview mirrors, sometimes dried brown blood. Open on lives like houses split by a tornado. Such a violent cemetery has more ghosts. Speeders—they ranged far; they gave Dee her wisdom. I wasn't allowed out of the car because of the rats.

Everything was hopeless. There was one hope, that animals could speak and would, to me, and that was crushed. I never meant to replace her or him. I could never be him, the parts were too heavy; I needed her too much. Still, I wanted something.

The film is "home massage for health" and it is showing in the old Sandusky Theater, with half the seats overturned and springs hanging out. Everyone nowadays goes to Columbus for movies. I am only here for Dee Coo Dah, who made the documentary. In the film she and other women, all naked from the waist up, are massaging people covered with blankets. Suddenly I realize I am watching her masturbate a man, her hands moving under the white blanket, her bare back to us. I don't understand. The Sandusky was never that kind of theater. Behind me I hear my father, breathing heavily.

Here among the mounds and oak trees there's no thought of whether doors are allowed to be locked or even shut. Everywhere else, the body's ownership is in question. Here, the voices in the hum can be recorded on a small cassette, and played back, over and over, until out of the static emerges a high-pitched voice speaking in several languages at once, and 99% of the time it is someone's mother. Here among the mounds, I don't worry over whether he will pounce or whether he will walk away and leave me.

Dreams run counter to your best inventions. I paste a lemur in profile, one dismayed dark eye, over the invention of the guillotine "the grandeur of the spectacle will attract many more to the place of execution...the criminal will approach his death boldly, enabled to face the blade of eternity." All the t's jump out, black, delicate sharp descending serifs, they won't surrender to the surrounding type. No one wants to read that, I can hear my sister say.

I edit the text as I dream, removing an em space from between each word my sister stutters in outrage and replacing it with an en space, one at a time. There are a lot of names, some of them men's. I erase them. Remove the word 'sister' wherever I find it. Dreams run counter to your best intentions. Whereas writing is lying as confession is lying. You intend a meaning no one can own. Writing is seduction as seduction is revenge. An alphabet of little dancing men.

But that belongs to an earlier time. I write for women. A blunt, egotistical, oceanic voice sweeping away all points of view. I write for women. I hear my sister sniggering at this, laughing out right.

Snow is falling out of season onto the surface of the lake.

Boats curved white mounds over invisible treacherous caverns. Rat the size of a dog, or is it a dog, or a horse? Swims out from under the dock in straight line, between my legs, pointing north to the center of the lake. Pointing with antlers. Deer swimming out to the center of the black lake then in a huge curve back to the shore a half-mile further up. This is true, I say, to convince her, you, that the world is worth living for in order to describe, and not some fiction I invent to delude myself. But even from a distance the sister can drain the image of its majesty. She wants to impoverish me. If all I had left was a cup of 27 coffee beans, or a page of a book with the words 27 coffee beans, she would tell me I had 26. And neither of us would be able to read the same number twice. Words can wound your words, virus-like, wear thin the cells of the spinning spheres inside you that organize your breathing and desires, bleed them dry and scatter the husks.

In the spring, thin black slime things come out of the walls, much smarter than slugs, they know when you enter a room and they move, fast. Smash them the room fills with an unbleachable stench.

Two young French sisters of Montpelier knew how to perform and excelled in the science of music. As they chanted according to the straight path they fused with the higher entities, and their souls ascended. See how god rejoices at hearing a tune done correctly and how much power there is in good music?

You have to find some kind of power of your own. By the time you want her, you have forfeited the privilege. You exploit whatever privileges you can discover. Christmas on earth. Peace on earth. You could never stand the thought of ascending.

Your sister hides the horse in the night, playing a game, and then goes away forever and you never. To find it again, you must swallow twenty volumes of the Book of Knowledge. With relief you see it is written in Hebrew, you can't be expected to read as well as swallow. Swallowed whole, the vowels climb up, become longer, then turn backward, and the sheen awakens and craves with fondness and great love. All the spheres have women's names and are restored to the power of speech, vision, retribution, justice, lesbian love.

Your sister is asleep. You ask her what she's doing. "Reading a book." What book? "Napoleon's Mare." What's it about? "You know. You wrote it."

Cavalier. Cavalry. When you enter another with longing and will, you are in a dark trapped place full of shadows not your own. This is not a place you can change by merely opening the curtains. Reaching in a hand. You begin writing her story to live up to her fear.

Say you seduced her. I can hear her screaming at this. Nothing has changed. She is the final authority. She is the authority on cruelty. Your invasion was complete and continuous.

A red pony with a mane of creamy white and a tail that touched the ground. Your sister was afraid of riding, but you forced her. Back in Cricket's field behind the row of blackthorns, you swatted her legs with an ironweed stick, the vibrating purple flower still attached. You can't resist her terror. She tells this story to her children before they fall asleep. Low, rocking, she tells them about the time you hid a noose of rope under loose straw and lured her into the barn, saying, "I made you something out of straw." A hat, she thought, a cowboy hat. Until the rope jerked tight around her leg, you loved her so, and knocked her flat.

A furious creature inside you began to exteriorize. In the pond you made her play horse—wrapping your legs around her and telling her to buck, buck, now rear up. Does she have an inner tree to reconnect the consonants with the vowels? Is she afraid of the powers of the body? Can you see the traces of the path you carve on their bodies?

Since then you have learned restraint. Though you are still writing her story. How do you stop a body from feeling triumph, seeking solace, hurting, hurting back, being curious, breaking, forgetting, wanting effect?

The powers of the body were greater than your understanding. Assaulted on all sides. You made the body a shell, a suitcase, an emblem of independence. Sometimes effective against the seeking out of your sentence.

I am a wanted man, mired in misfortune, hunted by both the law and my killer. Another man takes me in—kind, clean striped shirt in mint and white, a broad, plain face. Kisses me tenderly. I wish I could stay, tell him the truth. He would drive me out. Never stay anywhere long. Never return. In the night hear the doorbell. Already gone. Running down a dark path in a suburban wood. (Even when the suitcase doesn't appear, its absence is significant.)

My crime follows me everywhere, even if I change my

gender. Where all fears flow to shore. Stop thinking in north or south. Sheen works better than thinking.

I glue a postcard of The Horse With the Longest Mane in the World. Dapple blue Arabian mare with a silver white mane and tail that trail on the truckbed and lift in the wind like a veil. Onto "dragged him to an ambulance from the steps of the Palais de Justice and kept in solitary and forced to submit to the sleep cure."

Right now there are people sailing in the snow. A Chinese woman in a bucket floats by carrying a sign: I am map. I am under death.

After the flood of 1978 an entire telephone pole went by, bobbing and trailing its wires—still squeaking with disconnected voices. Suitcases, floating by like a family of ducks or the baggage of a trip that has finally escaped the family. A blouse with neck and wrist jewelry still attached in great heavy clumps, as if the upper headless half of a woman had sundered herself from the other criminal parts and jumped. Chains of silver fishes with moveable heads, a choker shaped like a snake, aqua-marine beads, and the rags of a silk blouse in grey-green, lavender paisley. I lobbed it onto the shore with a stick along with a stray tampon, a styrofoam cup, and a tiny plastic white horse with three legs. Another time a two-inch high rubber diver with helmet cage, fins, and harpoon.

I list or glue some jetsam to my sister in Athens, Greece. She sends back notes on the backs of bills, once an empty envelope, a black mouth that opened saying, "You thought you were so perfect. You brought our family down. You made our father sick. You placed yourself above our mother,

you supplanted her. You never noticed me. You took up all
the space with your histrionics, your stagey rebellions.
There were years where even the absence of your name was
a thundering wound at our table, years when for you I had
ceased to exist. Why did you leave us like that? Despising
and superior."

One day she writes that she has fallen in love with a cantor,
has no guilt and is writing again. The postage stamp is a
copper lion devouring a silver horse, or a horse emerging
from the straining jaws of a lion. Below the HELLAS in the
corner, a small bronze fox watches with an expression of
profound vicarious satisfaction. It is pasted over a yellow
strip of newsprint "when asked in court if it was a crime for
a woman to have lovers, Gabrielle Russier was told, 'the
quantity matters.' "

I am Map. Did she mean to say Nap? Sleep? Your sister will
bear a child who will name herself after a book your sister
dreamed you wrote? Did she mean Maat, vision? But why
the P? Tower, blasting. Or did she mean, pack your bag,
follow the wavery black lines around the world. Or, if you
had a home, would you need a map? Are you a conquering
army? Are you unknown territory? Are you bridled and
ready to go? Hot and slick, precarious, feeble as a bird
perched on your back. Smell of trampled juniper rushing
by, the grey magnetized clouds. Over raspberry hedges feel
how high her heart lifts. Swollen with pride in your speed
and grace, your muscles move beneath her, answering the
slightest pressure of her knees with a surge of motion, a
sheen of heat.

Can we claim to read it right? What she needs, what she wants, what she thinks she doesn't get. When whatever happens seems to have to. Motion holds no form for wise directives. Here comes Sorrel, holding out. Whispers say your time has passed, I ignore them. Even I don't know what I will, or how explain it. Hardly physical. Convoluted past untangling. The juror followed Mary many times, his strange ringed eyes. A tangled fascination. Bog braids, caked in mud and dried and tangled with the blindfold all these years. Put a surricote, standing erect, its harem eyes staring, proving again the superfluity of the extra in extra-terrestrial. Glue it on the smooth green lawn by the white ball where it can watch them scatter like newborn planets. Mary took a break. We played pool. The juror mentioned something about money and a Jew. She threw her pocket change against his chest. We left. We left but this is crazy. Nothing was said before or after. Of course that can't be true. But since there was an injured party. Words once spoken had to disappear and did. We drank gin. We took trips for art. We made movies in the sewer plant. Drenched by rain a sweatshirt faded pink and streaked with porch paint. What does it have to do with a claim, rising now unwanted dense untidy? Is it a crime to claim to have forgotten? Or, no. To have staked no claim. It's raining now.

A llama white and soaked is being led from out the subway.
Why so secretive so indirect? Try, try saying something
plain. Ok. Ok, I liked to kiss her more in public. He followed
her in public. I was already gone away. Where was her
protection? Now am I expected to explain, what's more, to
pay? Ok. In private, well, I can't claim to have been very
present. Though I couldn't put it down. Now, to the price.
It gets paid, it gets between. I still wear it.

Is it true I was absent? What is the half-life of a lie? If the
shape is vague, is any harm done it justified? I only lied
about how deep it went. It went as deep as you can imagine.
Taking years to return. I wasn't absent, I was right there,
living in my eyes, living in the newsprint where he did it.

A leopard is glued over "electric screwdriver, because, she
told police, he cheated her out of her mother's farm." She
looks over her shoulder, her spots arranging our griefs. Her
spine so curved. A form emerging from fear. A woman
lifting a red-edged white china cup in an airport or movie.
Jamaica. Mascara. Look. Just do me that one favor. The
purplish cast to the mahogany wall behind her, to the cat's
roan spots, to the woman's red lashes. The same qoph falls
on them all. Though there is fog enough to ground any
wirey thing. Just keep looking. Straining to see into fog. That
will be us, approaching. Why should you be scared? As I
child I was cared for by dark. Safe as a charcoal collar. Soft
speckled wolf and the belt that hooks with a twist to the left
same as the buckle on a horse's cobalt blanket, steaming
blue steam. Colors arranging our sorrows. Still shoveling
gravel too young crushed by the size of things in the sun.

Airport all fogged in. Montreal diverted to Prestwick. Have
you ever been jealous? In the days you recorded? In the

recording days? Past the B, magician. Past the O, no more excuses. Past the A, a fool walking blind. Past the C, corridor, Coaly-bay the outlaw horse. Her helplessness in the face of the unremembered. A dark green shade through a window. Where do you want to go? Prestwick. Montreal. I've chosen her only because she happened to be looking for a biographer.

Here is a map to distract you in your disintegration. Just a map. You wander, your eyes are occupied. While inside another self is forming. You need a map to distract you from straining to be. Through the window she turns off the green lamp and turns on another, nearer to us. This one is pale rose apricot. She picks up a yellow phone to call the police. Hey. We aren't thieves. We tear out, drive fast, need gas. How I became a watcher. An old guy's face sneers by outside, says "are you a museum?" Caught, she says, "no, a director." They grab her. I trap them in the bathroom with a rake and a broom. She gets away. We get away so far. You're allowed a little dog. I take four relative strangers. Dogs herding deers. Dogs in barrels. Dog statues on a barren island. What can you describe that isn't shattering or contained? Escaping or memorial? What can you do with only two colors? And then one of them has to be yellow or orange. Forsake the sun. Keep the earth, but at a distance, dangling, pendant. A shimmering copper green taffeta color.

The moon, the so-called future, is an authentic mystery. What is the trouble? Don't be put off. Don't listen just look around. Tell me if anything I say is painful. Shout. The so-called past changes far more rapidly than the future and with richer mystery. With increasing affection. I was born and resolved to always attempt the impossible. Now I had found another one impossible to love, to love. Making the

body supple as dressage, stretching to please and to bend
and to hang in the air, all four hooves suspended for a
second. And the coat milky as water at night. Have you ever
swum in the dark with a horse in a pond?

Now a crowd of people searching the autumn field for
parts. So large, beating resounds in everybody's living
rooms, but invisible, minus its object. If there is a body they
are going to find it. Tents and telephones set up in the field
where last seen. If there is a heart still beating they are going
to stop it.

I am watching Sorrel sing into a spoon. A forelock like a
quarterhorse. Now lights all over the twilight November
hill. They still think the body died. It breaks, but its knowing
core retreats to the eyes. I am watching her through fog but
about to love, always. This tilt brings on a copper green
taffeta screen. Have you grieved, have you been sent home?
Do voices tell you when to pack your bag? The heart is a
muscle. Everything real is invisible. Colors only sharpen. I
got away but I had to get somewhere. No one was looking
very hard. They look harder for bodies in canals. I went to
upper Michigan but there under the dock were her wet
black lashes clumped and piercing.

In the morning I am wakened in a houseful of women by a
man who has to check the furnace. Later in the kitchen she
says do you get attached? And what do you think of
faithfulness? And I don't know how to love. Someone says
all mammals growl. Another says drumming for peace and
I am thinking drumming! Peace! I'll throw her family
crystal against the wall. Seconds later the walls begin to
shake. Crystal wineglass rimmed in red dives sorrowfully
off an edge. I think the furnace man planted a bomb in the

houseful of women. It was a significant earthquake. Other local people had different theories. "I thought it was my wife, rocking too hard." Wife: "I thought it was me, I ate too much."

This shaking destroys my semblance of a new life. No steadfastness. You have to be ready to look at all at once, not shackled to this particular light, not punishing two years ago with darkness. See two figures on a street in Philadelphia. Rose Lane, Flourtown. Standing in front of a grey stone house which has shrunk to the size of a doll's even though I never really stood before it in a body. It is always spring when the tear begins its rip. Is a rupture a process or too sudden for that noun? Doesn't everything have to exist in time? When I saw the house, from miles away, in a room full of its remainders—puppets under the bed, heavy main-line furniture—the house was bigger. I saw it through her eyes. Which proves when you look at the past your eyes revert to the height from the ground they were when they were looking. And when you look through the lover's eyes you may be any age, you may see yourself vanish, before or after, sooner than you planned. Therefore a rupture is a process out of time. Out on the sidewalk, she said, "Come back soon. Wear your wet suit." I never saw her again, though I could have. Or I could now if I swam in her direction.

A documentary of watching without hope. Voices without mouths. No one maps this territory without pathos or persuasion. Trying to say it will pass or it will never pass. No one can stand to be suspended in the uncertainty. Reflected in the square window is a porthole window in the door to the road under the hill below the highway. Through the first window are lights from the other side. You may try to contact the other side while you are waiting and they may answer with pronouncements both soothing and dire. If they weren't invisible we wouldn't believe them. We'd operate. And under the water between here and the other shore I was swimming sometimes colliding with the hard flank of a fish or the sticky side of a muskrat, stroked from beneath by a thousand swaying weeds, tingling slightly with electricity, little shocks, weed syllables, to the isolated body. In isolation voices pour out of every orifice.

Delusion flourishes in isolation (as it does in pairs) spawning wanton entities. A Mormon hears a voice telling him to bomb his church. A woman hears a voice telling her to render him back to his maker. A couple is led to the northernmost tip of Michigan to freeze in their car waiting for the extraterrestrial. I am partial to the voices that speak in static and the pens that write in boxes. I too think of the voice as a benevolent secret will. So often a whisper will start things moving on my behalf. Female, of course. Gaia. Creatrix.

But here in this quaking farmhouse fog I know, because every crevice is filled with despair. The voice that tells me whatever happens, happens for the best. No matter how miserable, how damaged. Manipulates me. Rises maniacally out of stinking rubble, the rotten cabbage bed. Voice of the christian, the scientist, the resigned, the faithful. Voice of the snake handler, ever hopeful, bit for the last time, voice of the Everly brothers in Marilyn March's pink teen bedroom singing I'll never leave you, the kind of angel echo that scars your years. Voice leading the Tollund bog woman into the fen. "We must suppose she was led blindfolded into the bog." Must we suppose? Tonight in the farmhouse, pink lamps, old rose rug, mice, crickets, someone cooking anguish over a stove, I know the voice is not innocent is not spirit moving through vessel. Has no authority. Don't listen to me, it is saying, don't trust anything you hear. Becoming thus even more desirable. Amoral voice, sly voice. From across the swamp a donkey of the equivalent age of 64, his red-rimmed eyes sunken in a head that is unnatural enough to be worn on stage, named after our fathers, scronks his inexhaustible craven need into the night. I think, my oracle is calling, needs me so. I gather his cries.

So what. The infinite surprise of words, their inexhaustible swell. Their relentless subversive circling. Interesting as a condition. Images I never would have thought of, descriptions of places I've never seen. Dark green walls, sucking a red and white peppermint? "*Yes*, that's him in his study." A sideboard with two candles? A green park bench with a metal label and two bolts? "Yes, how could you know?" Reading a big thick book, author starts with m? "Yes, in the hospital, Marquez." A circus without a sky? "Yes! Chicago! in the coliseum! when I was six!"

How can you resist a circus without a sky? C: slow moving hierophant of the animal world. I: trumpeting her vision of hell. R: upper left vacant sphere, unseated, unthroned, causing all the trouble. C: coded movements in the drums keeping her up in the air. U: you, translator. S: fate or iron, red and flaky, sucked up from Cricket's well. When the edges blur, the substance can really travel.

Rustling of hay, a horse named Cricket bangs her rubber bucket. It became increasingly hard to discern who was speaking. I began to feel I was entering a vast echoing chamber of intuitions, random observations, reverberations.

Try the back door. Put it on a list to remember to fear for your
safety. Cut short the last long revery. I believe in the rapid
joining of leather without hands; in a word forming from
static composed of syllables in Czechoslovakian, Latvian,
Greek; in objects passing unharmed through bodies years
later. I believe it. Mary said all the Japanese horses flew off
the shelves to the left. They grabbed each other, Mary and
her photographer, by the upper arms as the earth tried to
buck them down. It's an earthquake, said the one with the
camera. No, she said, it's too big, it must be something we
ate. All our conversations begin and end with horses.

Try the back door it never did lock. He cut the phone lines
and cut their throats while they lay in their beds. If you never
lie down they can't cut the cord. Put on your list to check
your door. Because two more were stabbed age 60 age 90.
A rupture doesn't exist in time. This present moment must
explode in horror or it isn't me speaking, it will take me by
surprise. I write you to be convincing. Speaking from the
vast reaches of otherness in the oracular cave of the brain.
You do this you do that. You arrange for pain. Arrange for
love, if that is what you want. Not easy, if you've arranged
to be destroyed nightly. Cut short that last scenario, where
all comes due and you pay and you pay. Turn the loving eye
on your own movements in water, arms alive hair astray.
Nothing else was disturbed. Only the Japanese horses, and
they settled slightly left of where they started, where you
are now still staring at your waves and willows a shocking
unnatural green. Cut short the last conversation before you
finish it for the one in trouble. It doesn't have to end with an
unlocked door inviting it to be yours.

And fast as it comes apart, words become deteriorated. All
around the menace sucks and cycles. Damage is rising and

you stay put. Like sisters you say and I freeze thinking of
years. No recovery. That bad? As bad as sisters? My sister
croons her children to sleep on tales of my abuse and
arrogance, a myth in the making, now to my niece Nap I am
the harpy that haunts her she longs to be. Do you mean the
kind of sisters who circle their pact? The kind that say yes
yes eyes locked in ever spiraling terror and fascination at
every passing bitter thought. Two of them lived down the
road with a bull and a terrier to protect them from traveling
men. Driving twenty in an old black Chevrolet one was
allowed to speak and one to steer. Of course the one denied
speech became the oracle. Now one is vomiting into a sink.
The other into the phone. Couvade. I cover my part. Coma.
Cannot remember her face, her sister's face. Fury makes its
target numb. Or freezes its prey. Though both feel prey to
conspiracy. This is a breakdown. Come out of it, look
straight at it. I knew there was a crime though not the one
hung on me. This was a wedge and somewhere spite drove
it. Numbly fury wrecks its fate against the thing that holds
its solace.

Forced entry collapses the means of entry, requiring with-
drawing to a more distant place from which to begin again.
Needles always out of sight, stimulate a line from Venus to
Mars to its little outburst. Its brave boyish charge. There it
was. You're right about the fury. A terrier charging a bull,
that's how we all feel. Wrong about the needles. Who is
sticking them into who is the younger sister who is the one
stuck full and staggering. No one is. No one is. That was
then when everyone was bigger and could pin you down.
This is you behind the wheel and speak for yourself. Do you
think you have a right to utter outloud every bitter word
that passes by your eye? No one is keeping you from

speaking. You should have kept it to yourself. Instead you
had to keep the needles in it.

A woman in disintegration is washing windows. Am I in
the clear? A movement away is always a movement toward. The water waves south. The train carrying coal or
arms north geese trembling willow no stillness any place.
You speed, they take it away. No movement without
disintegration. In vain I roll under the tongues of my shoes,
too long, obscenely wagging. I roll under the cuffs of my
coat, fraying in the violent passing of years.

So fast as it comes apart, name it. Hypnotic rags in tatters.
Rags and tatters of the daughter of a Spaniard and an
Indian. Here she is in the eggs and peppers. Madonna-blue
plastic blowing in the cow field, becoming natural, becoming its own evidence. Nothing moving to me in the whole
cloth.

Today they shaved the horses. Tridents, top hats, four leaf
clovers breaking up their winter coats, for polo they say or
else they say for the blankets (hair rubs). She shoots out, the
mare with her furious lips, ears, a thin film of rage dropping
over her eyes. Here, as we are, to break into pieces, to bleed,
to rail to gain a new perspective? Surely there must be more
for her. Always assume your rage has reason (to bring you
nearer) the bay has her reasons rock the planet.

I grind slaked lime, ammonium chloride, cinnamon, clove
and charcoal. This is a powder blown in the eyes. When the
veil descends and the horse in her fury believes she is seeing
the caul of her mother's womb, blow softly on your dusty
palm, this powder restores her vision, drags her back to her

prison, where your love—you can't save them—bears feeble witness. Not religion.

I watched Detroit burn from the rooftop safe in the arms of women anesthesiologists. The movement in and out of death is expensive. All the colors in a flame, the pull of home, oblivion, under the brain. The movement away— perpetual comfort, ash wind tide the hissing sound of departure.

On the highway men stream drunk and murderous from the North Forty. When they come together I hear their women crying in the parking lot. A movement toward you would not have been possible otherwise. In Eve's unpaved plot would a wave move only to, never from? Shards breaking make a way. In the parking structure they leave a dark haired woman sprawled, undone, whiter than any-thing. When they moved on me, high school, football team as one body, in the parking lot of the bowling alley, their rage had reason. Sobbing in another lot after Sophie's Choice—the double fear of stretching and abandonment— hear the sound far away as a stick wrapped in soaking rags hitting a floor. Resignation. Anesthetic. Rhythmic. Heart beat. Remembering. Rising. In the neutral places, where you park, enter, leave their world, but the sobbing heaves up another buckle, another gouge, paved over.

Two figures through a screen. A June of a seventh year for insects. Cincinnati one hot thrumming copper body. Locust crowing drowning out every window fan. Down below he hits her. His rage has purpose. You hear a fist pounding her stomach the sound of a mop, sobbing. Her feet crunching the locust, a slam, her car's wipers scrubbing their bodies to white gold froth. She leaves you more alone. She comes back. Couldn't stop her. Studying pain. Disremembering.

The middle is Ohio. War born a great fondness. They know how to materialize without reason, hope without doubt. You have to admire in your speeding escapes. An image of Jesus has just been sighted on the water tower and alternate Tuesdays on the Rigg's garage door. Giant Bird Lifts Child Three Feet in Air, Coshocton, Ohio. Chillicothe, "Chill-i-coat," you call out, then embarrassed at mispronouncing, like someone who has never traveled, quickly tell me how your father insists on saying Chicago street names in the European way, even when he's lost, even when conceding would lead him home. But where did home go. All bars look like Europe. In Ohio they sight the unknown in the midst of the known, what do they know of Europe but peat and water, no great sadness. UFO's shaped like cigars. How hard can it rain and not wash away the insistent flat weeping comfort. A great sadness. Their sightings increase with extremes of weather. And whether or not it will save them depends a lot on the media. The world depends on the middle to mispronounce to sight and to send their ludicrous visions back to the weather back to seed the clouds in the craven Detroit streets where we all fled, Beaubien, bowbean.

Nineteen years later you choke. I see a man on the ridge above with a rifle. I am ready, in case I live, with a complete description. No, you say, it's a snake. There by the road a black and silver snake thick as a wrist frozen in a line toward freedom. Milk snake. Full of the elixir, green and white, the formula known to every hopeful shaman. That paralyzes you then melts your throat (you say the sound you make when you see a snake is the same sound you make when coming). You see a snake, I see a man taking aim. The heart

that wants to croon is spitting venom. As if you can choose
what to fear or hate.

All night I watch your hair, the waves tighten into curls. A
baby's fingers relaxing into a fist. Is there a word for this?
Yes, universe. Winding your best intentions with your
secret bent and bringing about selves beyond your invention.

Witness then. I can look at anything. The cost is stupefying.
A monk in flames, a woman left armless to die in the desert,
doesn't die, speaks his name. Something bloody crawling
along a trail. These have lodgings, demands. Turning desire
to hallucination. I hate them, look what they have done. I
have a passionate attachment to the world, in its inexorable
cruel revolution.

To shock, you say. I exploit words. How else propel oneself
out of the hills of stone women rocking on porches. Birdie,
Annabelle, Mary Claude, their voices stub up, help push
out my no against the future.

The elephant, cow, seal, absorb deep shocks to the body of
earth but women are not absorbers. Women are furious
they tear at themselves at each other. Some refuse this. For
some to tear is to refuse. Some elephants run renegade.
Outside the wind whips the water to spit.

When I come to you there is a them I drown in my wake, I
must pretend. The one who arrests you who takes it away.
Who calls you, plaintive, needy, across the separating years,
the ones who beat her up in the parking lot of the hospital,
the macha, when she tried to see her lover, who'd been
raped. Distance, you say, journalism. How is it possible to

take this staggering weight of bitterness and turn, wrench it back to its source. Lost in every paragraph. Visible only as the thin green string, the serpentine. A crack. The only place on earth still fertile. A cracked plate secret, widening. Exactly what they fear they bury us all for.

You say name your personal history. Is it 9 million pieces of scorched meat or is it one matchstick aimed at your arm. Stubborn, a veil of mucus descends from under the lid. A powder blown in the eyes. An amazement of grief spills out for a penny of rage. No one can tell me not to spend it. How to spend it.

Buy a plot as far away as possible. My great aunt Birdie who refused who made her 40 acres a bitter furrow. Do I want a homestead of silent resistance do I want the grave between your brows. So as to…be careful…of what I do not hate…to be above a rabid dog.

Above, you hold me. You hold me down. A stronger grip than my brother's, holding me under water. Warn her I don't want to hurt her she's making me want to hurt her. You? Hurt you? No is a scream screaming and clawing at a grassy violet mound in the Smokies and in the circus she lifts it over and over with her trunk and throws it on her own head, a hank of grass and earth. The stake, the rope, could be lifted out with as little effort but the stake is in the heart. That the heart can be speared and lifted out with so little effort and wrung like a rag.

You stand in the doorway, smoking. Cigarette makes her way to Algiers. A word in a novel becomes a slender body dangling on a dry spot between your lips or squeezed like a vise inside another body in the mouth they call oracle. And

finally I understand universe. Daleth, Venus, any open
door. Claws soften back into pads. Put your hand in the
serpentine it closes over softly, fear, as curious as we are. It
wants...it expects the worst but it still hopes for love. A
tender voracious creature.

Its other eye indicating stop. Please don't stop. With two
eyes in the face of every woman one will always betray her.
Probably the Uranus eye. Have you tried putting a patch
over it? Have you tried finding out what it needs? Venus of
course, a little compassion. So far in the back of the oracular
cave, so aloof and yet. This chestnut colored eye is not at all
objective. I can look at anything, all the drawings on the
wall. Scenes to blow apart the fragile organism lying like
crazy to live—I can look and I can come back to you. You in
the eye that withdrew, you still pay for something you had
no choice but to abandon. Stop paying. Take it up now,
waste no more time posturing. That's what you can't look
at, right? Not the woman in the desert with her arms cut off
but the woman looking at you, her arms held out to you.

I know a lot of things I can't express. Two refrigerators are
still speaking to each other in a field beside the newsprint
words: "I have no refrigerator no clothes. I have to start over.
Whole plains are rubble with only here and there an upright
refrigerator." I paste a labrador with pups between them, a
witness, a jury of dogs. "You think of yourself as part of
society but then something like a hurricane and you know
you are alone. Have to start over." This spiteful whisper
spoils things in advance. When she was nine, my niece
Napoleon said, "The most important thing is a person's job,
right?" "No," I answered, thinking of my cruelty to her
mother, "Being kind is more important." Oh her look of
tender outrage. Three years later still struggling valiantly to

rehabilitate me, Nap says, "Look, tell yourself you can do anything." She is stripping corn into a newspaper funnel for her black mare. "When I race, I say son of a bitch son of a bitch under my breath to keep my rhythm." I knew someone someday would break it. I knew who, I heard it whispered. The green cornsilk getting all inside her oxblood shoe polish hair. Increasingly difficult to discern who is speaking. I began stepping into a vast undifferentiated consciousness that simply felt like, well, me.

I write with the words that are already printed, there are plenty of words in the world. I paste the pictures with the words for which they are longing. I paste a boa down on the morning paper, a tender, voracious creature. The headline says, "Endicott kids are erasing themselves." "Using a pencil eraser, rubbing it near the knuckle, tearing away the skin, leaving it raw and bleeding." Leaving it forked and speaking. "Most of them are girls," it says.

There are 38 snakes in a pile. I made this living pyramid. They hook on to each other and weave. Then they say I have to move this stack two feet over. How can I move it. You cannot move a pyramid of snakes. They shoot off in all directions, into any orifice. I always try to do the impossible.

Four timber rattlers and a rose copperhead spill from a white pine box in the full gospel jesus church of Columbus, Ohio. And these signs shall follow them that believe; they shall speak with new tongues they shall take up serpents.

His whole arm split open from shoulder to elbow, he waited for fate to reveal itself. I paste photos of him with his face in a pillow of snakes, stuffing snakes into his shirt. Slain in the spirit.

They pressed me. The ether rose. Making strange. Ecstatic babble. I took my own sacred texts as anti-gospel and changing the pronouns back, my head on a pillow of snakes, reached my arms in there, waiting for fate to reveal herself.

I asked my father is the snake church still on High Street? Closed down, he said. Hank got bit and died. And the factory women? Do their skirts cease to whirl? Floats, settling, falling somewhere, back to Kentucky? Where they taught me all about serpents. Where the men eat first and the women suck in their lips, stub up. The gay ones cross the river to Cincinnati where she rocks them to sleep on riverboats. Some make their way north to Columbus, to the bars on High Street, nurses, anesthesiologists, their pockets full of snakes of every color.

There are three kinds of love: the kind that acts on the nerves and stops the breath, the kind that causes disintegration, the kind that destroys the clotting power of blood and lets the heart pour out through the wound.

You cannot move a pile of 38 snakes. I always set about the impossible. The possible is a lullaby. Why is it so impossible to love or shed a skin?

I want to know why they are erasing themselves. They say women are hissing in double tongues. I have the same question for eons. What exactly is wakening? And what is a comforting delusion? Protective coloration? Intimidation by display? And why are they erasing themselves?

So I try erasing the skin on the Saturn finger, the one where it all comes to earth, iron heaviness, iron tenderness. It works, it matches the raw unspoken thing, the way a phrase, a word, a letter, a sound, making a *mark* eases, contains, rearranges the various pains of the body, diseases, heart seizes. An alphabet of bursting longing, marking the body with sign *and* sensation. Shedding a skin, revealing another, mine, mine.

How many more days before the wound won't close it pulls the meat from the bone, this poison. Under the sternum. I said cavity. The snake said give me a home. So many times. How many times can you fall like that out of the world but in it. Slain in the spirit. Faith, spun of your own fierce pride, no one knows better how fragile. She said her hands go cold when she's ready. Sure I know that. Anytime you attempt beyond, you become amphibian, reptilian. There's no trick. You can't control a viper. Nothing to do with will or surrender. You pick it up it bites or doesn't. I said I was ready. So one day I said ok snake, enter. I knew all about kundalini.

I would be walking, early in the morning, steam rising from the lake and I would feel her uncoil begin her ascent. Mind trying to steer, saying oh no, not this again. Ok. You don't know where you are. Do you know your address? 8...8...8...? Your name? No. But you know if you keep on you will turn where you have to even though you don't know where you are going or why or what is this town anyway why is trash blowing in three directions, why is the water so brown, why are all the boats wrapped in plastic six colors of blue? Mind would go on like this, pretending to make meaning. And all the time she's rising and I'm shedding strings of personality stresses of the daily sheen via an unseizable nauseating wrench of—pleasure? So that when the foolish number breaks through triumphantly, 893, my old address, as if it mattered more than anything, I am changed. The day unrolls same as the one before but I enter it through another word. Sounds and their images set free. Ana acetylene anesthesia anathema. My father shooting blue fire on metal lit from below and masked, Mary going under once again to the needle, Sorrel screaming at a frozen snake, Nan immune to anesthesia, immune to pain, immune to authority, cutting, sewing, anathema the scarlet A, the death keen anathema marantha, serpents or pricks swinging from her apron, anath, rouged and hennaed, wading in blood...

To the same degree. Mat chinoi. Thus was my body seethed as in a pit. Violated not in the condensed body/womb, but slain in the spirit.

They say no snakes have a true voice. They can only rub things together. I give them the printed word with which to hiss their message to women. In the serpentarium a 78-year-old man was bitten 148 times, last by a Pakistani pit viper. No apologies. Would *he* have said he was obsessed with sex? Would *he* have said he sometimes wished to die? Would *he* have taken to erasing the skin from his hands?

I paste the simple garden variety over the words "One girl, age twelve, rubbed the skin off right in front of me. She said, 'I like the pain.'"

And they spin and they croon and scream. They gag they reach back for the syllables. Death is in the snake box. Don't go in the box unless death is with you. Every action, object, or thought. Grace enters through open syllables. Lie down with me and let grace enter. Out of the countryside, draping their arms, twisted into living bundles on their heads.

There are two defenses against love: intimidation by display, intimation of demise. Arrange and distribute your colors like the gaboon viper, the river jack, purple, crimson, rose, silver, yellow, russet and black, shape shifting. Stripe your skin with your own inscription.

Because her venom causes paralysis. A paralyzing effort, to hold an image of a window without shame, of the light finding you, against the image of the one who waits in shadows. Anna O. became paralyzed...became unparalyzed by speaking in tongues. Become the venomous tongue. Become the subversive syllables under sense. Paralysis. Peristalsis. The peculiar snakelike wave motion of the intestine, successive contraction of the walls, forcing up the shudder, the flash...

A chartreuse snake goes over the words "rescuers were forced to abandon the search." Means: forego hope here. That is a prerequisite. Hope has silenced you. Replace with accuracy. Focus same intensity of hope on getting the picture clear. Same urgency to counter despair but different focus. From being seen to seeing.

Seeing a red snake, curved swath on rough black. In its arches, two dots, part of a charm against intruders? Gravel. A young girl, 16, is sitting on the floor before a full-length mirror, in the bald light of a ceiling bulb, the better to see every movement of blood in the veins. Firm legs spread, a line of tan at the top, white torso, sunburnt arm reaching in, veins in hand moving under the skin. She notes how the stomach spreads at this angle, the torso is a white truce flag, the throat growing a purplish patch. She notes the eyes want to close, they recede, they glint, they grow red behind green, they look ferocious. She keeps them open. Watches to the end several nights, exorcizing shame, practicing being seen.

On the last night she moves through the house turning off the lights. Down by the line of blackthorns, two figures start across the yard. Moves through the dark house to her bedroom, through the room to the window to follow the figures. To the gap where, carelessly (complicity finds its first crevice here) she has not drawn the curtain all the way. To the three-inch gap of night, view of horse field, five acres of blue summer grass. No stars out this window, a strange opacity forms slowly, as slowly as a season, into two faces pressed close. Then slowly into two known faces. Screams, screams their names. Her father runs into the night, shirtless, marine gun stuck in pocket. Spurting his rage to each of their fathers. Neighbors, they make their honorable pacts.

In the morning she examines the ground beneath the window, grass flattened, worn from more than one night, from many nights of being seen. Several days later a giant spray-painted sign appears on the blacktop lane in front of her house: two dots and a snake with two humps, red— breasts.

Restores me to my sentences. The sacred text obviously must be forked: what she didn't want, what she wants, what she may not live to see. I have her skin, white and ripped, woven through my doormat. Shed for me. Who is calling? Snake your trail is hard to follow. Your fluid grace is hard to bear. She brings you to me, by her merciless dilation. You bite, I pretend to fall. Pulls the flesh from the bone. Writhing. Like any common mystic. Brings the flesh back to life on the bones, the touch of a hand on a throat across the centuries of speechlessness.

I dream you say forklift. This is something a snake can do with its tongue. It also means put four fingers in you. But instead I'm putting pieces of words inside, some syllables italic some roman. Named écriturisme by a French pastry cook who invented two parallel alphabets in icing sugar, who said "all is words" and, drawing with both hands at once, binah and hokmah, was able to describe the meaning of the universe. But here I am sending a jagged zigzag line of syllables slanting in different directions into you, pushing, pulling you, sending you off through all the levels of the realm.

Four women are suffering, suffering their fate. On a train between life and its subject. Writing their vertigos, their bile—all night they regale with their plight a small boy dressed in tartans.

Their hour is receding. Four women lounge, condemned together to eat grass—a family would poison their bread. They have a hand-out of places of interest to their kind of women in Montreal. "Restaurants" lists one—followed by the word sandwiches. But the train is quatre-vingts à l'heure. It is faster than they can write or swallow.

My color is ordinary. I am negligible. Their symptoms mimic love. I promise a short cure. I decide my taste will find its grave in our destination.

The four wear obscene perfume, impudent white shirts, blinding. The four superimpose their baggage on a plank and descend, haggling silently. I'm in an embarrassed compartment. It is necessary that I travel in order to hear in a corner what I desire for my soul. Dear soul, they always make you a place.

The four women who have the advantage of vocabulary,

their conversation is all broccoli, good for the fever, bad for the fever. A society of wise women manquée.

She is alone on the quay. Here, below us in the ravishment. She always has to be different. As a child she would furiously decorate the scraps out of which the ginger man was cut. Hundreds and thousands around a hole void arms and legs outstretched. She named boys bikes bikes and girls bikes ball bikes imagining the missing bar to be space for the delicate male appendages. She hasn't time to clean up the mess of her book. Her eyes ice us sometimes, saying, "Four indistinguishable birds. One doesn't judge birds." She doesn't consider birds animals, but things to be scattered, things that perch obscuring the words on the walls. The woman she loves, whose parole she refuses, won't say goodbye. We aren't absolved. We come and go en masse.

I begin my cure with elevation. Her face from here as clear as Squeaky's the day before the failed attempt. All my dreams are failed attempts or magical animal combinations. I don't forget her. I watch her lose herself among the others from the chimney. I have watched from the highest smokestacks of jealousy, smut covered, dogged. I can overlook a lake and speak calmly. My feeble cure that didn't last a term. My chewing of books, my caress of the same table bumping into the same hard surface where I once wrote beside a waterfall in the book mill (in my mind) paradise. Actually—

She jumped up because another had entered, spelled her, departed smartly. Jumped up to go read the titles the other had been perusing. On the discount table. Where they all sit squashed spine up visage to hidden visage as passengers on a train to Montreal.

My cure opens wide green eyes. Pardons the nervous ticks.
Has attended enough spectacles of elocution to be able to
quit the study of mouth movements. The cure divorces me
from the human voice. It devours the faces of strangers, the
names of new drugs, the faces of friends. The name of a
thing becoming a more powerful drug than the thing.

She had, when born, hands that wrote crazy as the moon
one or the other, clacking against the other, applause as
graceful as the predicament of chairs (accepting butts). This
young woman, or when she was young, she predicted the
art of the XIIIe siecle, before it was explained. Its design. Her
voice was a translation of moose, of interior travail in dark
woods of madness and independence from vocal communal
tradition and pride in pissing halfway up the side of a barn.
In the undulating line of her brow, beggars are there. But
they don't hesitate to choose the universe over her inventions. We tire of her too. Comfortable train, for getting from
pool of light to bedside lamp. We tire of her and her
chargeable batteries.

I decided to hole up in Dolgelly without falsifying my
signature. I wrote, I waited for notes from the days to come.
Through an open window or transom. I heard water running under everything. Part of my cure, I mined its benefits.
I tried to speed the future back by enacting anything I or
they dreamed I did. If they dreamed I ate a dirty carrot, I ate
one now. Finally jettisoned by my notes, I left under a sweet
outraged rain. What scent storm waters give to a page. Men
under a tree laughed but they were the ones in danger.

Because of all that moving I lashed myself to one menu:
tomato, laughing greens, menial chocolate, inferior blended

scotches. I docked at a calm veranda. Arriving on foot, taken aboard a city chained to its toilets, working for awhile in tar, that's how I passed through the indifference of love. I killed the conductor. A car full of tourists stopped, the conductor had crossed their wishes. They thought they were accident. It was me. We were a long time in that hand. I wanted to sing of the menthol condition to loosen us all. We were in that hand and then worse, we separated, like shocked marbles. I was again someone, not fate. Not an entity called two times two, born of their foursquare traveling arrangements.

We finally find a restaurant in the meat district the leather district going straight to the heart of hatred and difference. We eat Caesar salad, speaking of new drugs for depression. Next to us a man lines up seven bottles of pills, pours a pile of pills from each, makes a chinese checkers of red, blue, green capsules and begins to swallow them one pill one sip of white wine.

When I entered the cafe-hotel-restaurant the peas rolled toward my table. Why isn't this Wales? When I asked the writers, they said but your mountain is here, not abroad. Not outloud but with their lips their bent chewing heads. Tomb and avalanche. I like mystery but I hate hints. I hate sculpture. The third dimension. I hate menus. I didn't want a mountain. I couldn't understand why they wouldn't give me the answer I wanted. It's possible they were other, they were writing their books mentally, in public. I hated them. I wanted to smack their heads with a tubafore.

Their strained kindness, confused, as if a plan should have arisen by the mere convergence of four suitcases in the same customs cubicle. I had cold blood. Punished by disappointing architecture and stalls of portrait hawkers in bell bottoms.

Coffee with sugar. On a bench I watched the train that always approached. Then, left.

Surrounded by mothers, I read in a book the words of women writers and journalists. One had a horror of a triangle of cheese on paper money. A fifteen-year-old religious sat facing me in the now compartment and smacked my knee. I wondered for a long time why she tried to provoke me. I called her the dirty girl (in my mind). She was very beautiful, a brunette Brigitte Bardot. I emptied my sack of crackers to her. Stop staring, bitch, she said. When the four were children they were granted permission to spend the night in the shark room of the San Francisco Aquarium. They took four sleeping bags and the ouija board. At 1:35 it spelled BITCH. They rolled up and ran home.

Four women, again, are trying not to be moved by nostalgia. Trying to improve their look, then release it casually into the public air with an attitude of detachment. Important to note they wore everything they carried, eventually.

They were booked on a street called Wolf in a guest house called the Hunter where rows of men stared out from under their shaven polls in silence, why wasn't I warned when I pronounced the French to my mother and she translated it into the familiar benign void where nothing like that happened in Ohio or her books and those magazines were buried by her papa under Life. So often she had tricked me to trust oblivion.

Four women have to talk corners like pool. I could understand how three times three was born in the subconscious of Cox and burst upon that circle of sitters with a voracious if inaccurate voice. Offering beer to nondrinkers scallops to

noneaters, warning of bull dykes, trying to enter the life of
the flesh by proxy and landing in the wrong circle, again.

One dallied on the morning of her birthday and said to the
others to tie this white handkerchief outside breakfast go up
St. Denis. But alas they went down and their flag a white
storm signified nothing. So my father tries to signal me
down the years making dumb erratic gestures that I copy
uncomprehending. The three ate eggs and coffee, refills cost
more. The other night he climbed to fix the whole disintegrating superstructure and fell slowly turning greyer,
postponing the final splat by bumping softly down a series
of convenient ledges, 13, 16, 21, 26, 37, 40.

Four women are as stable as table legs. Even so, brief
desperate triangles will insist in an effort at momentum,
before one of the women makes herself into a ledge.

I believe this is the answer to table levitation. To have four
legs is a terrible thing. Look at the fate of stable horses, veal
calves, first children of two. Everything wants to be three,
then they can roll into a stunning, superior circle. With the
combined energy of our minds and coffee and the unspent
writing building up in our polite muscles, we focused on
lopping off a leg.

We watched a corner begin to sink. Frantic, she searched
every pocket, pulling out fistfuls of bad wrong paper never
the train ticket. Brightly as nurses we helped her search,
pressing lightly on her head.

We think it was these mental efforts at asymmetry that
caused two times two to materialize and being describing.

The breakfast table rocked to and fro with a gentle craving, scooted, hopped, rose three feet above the waitress. Suddenly visible, I continued trying to read French while praying never to translate truthfully. When you understand electricity, the difference between spectral light and pigment, table levitation, there is so little left of mystery. No one has even ever seen a wormhole so there's no point chasing after that with a notebook.

We quit the Hunter for another pornographic platform slightly west of here. The bath is in the room a shiny divider of black tile swans frosted in a mirror. One can sit on the toilet and see herself reflected above the bath. Above the head of the one in the bath, at the same time as the one in the bed can see the bath and the toilet sitter. A ledge covered the toilet sitter to the shoulder. But not if you are the size of a human, only if you are a small dog. This way you can entertain someone comfortably lounging on bed, bath (jacuzzi), toilet, or entering as if to a party through the door. That is, if they get by the hostile Pakistani woman. This is important because two of us are having unfortunate birthdays. Otherwise, outside it is chairs gutted and spilling dirty foam and needles underneath watchers and people with dirty feet.

We find a better room with a whiter landlady in an older house with higher ceilings and no exposed wires windows that open above a silent jazz bar across from an ecology bookstore. We know where we are. From our window we can see bottled water. We have newspapers announcing cultural events that have, fortunately, just ended. We have a toilet with a door. Above the bar remembered fondly.

This is the bar? This is the bar with aquarium for eels we

heard so much about one snowy night last Christmas? But now we hear a different story. It was not the right bar, the bar of renown, and we were miserable then too. Only time and words weave green-black eels confined in a stagnant box with nowhere to hide or write into love at second sight. Atmosphere can never be truly appreciated firsthand. The romance recedes from us as it must, into the unanswered phone ringing in the high ceilinged room of a lucky permanent alien we once knew but don't want to see. Into the *other* women's bar. Every apartment, we have been told, has a clawfoot bathtub with a woman writer floating in it, smoking. We begin dreaming of the Adirondacks. Green plaid rugs beside fires, looming peopleless forests. We arrive still alive in the forest and turn a long time before entering the cars that take us into the shadow. The next morning

They pit themselves one against the other in silence. They offer a beautiful place elsewhere they haven't seen but pretend to have visited. I am disinfected after each transport. I return to an impermeable blue coldness in the chest six o'clock in the morning. The artistic detours that are supposed to make material bloom into the sensual, I know their true function. To disappoint. To enliven the imagination of the perpetually dissatisfied reader who must live inside her head. I like my green jacket the shredded map in pocket. I like the way my hair stands up on one side because I accidently doused it with shampoo instead of hair tonic. I talk to my coffee and it doesn't answer politely. It tells me to go, go, go.

We have turned our heads against her. We have chased a look down and she is afraid now. She proposes detours, she imposes her love of objects, she finds endless convergences

on her tattered map. But she doesn't imprison us with her
arty destinations. We remain free because she is nonchalant;
we are in pain. Parading the streets looking for sweets,
thinking of our dissertations our novels our performances
our garden coffee table books, the noon sun is more than
equal to her concentrated presence. We're really here, we
say triumphantly. The streets sparkle. We hate her now
with unrelieved intensity which unites us into a glittering
frontage. The pulsar is actually what is left over after the
explosion, a dead body squeezed into a mass and starting
to move faster. To be entangled and to want to be free of
course forces separation, which binds. We pretend to private thoughts of traveling alone in future.

My dear ruptured voyages, my fractured routes, my missed
festivals, my subjects which I dictate that never finish or
return. I take distance from this dirty city, from autumn,
friendship. From the feminine style. Where style is sensibility,
stupefying documentation. You loved your teacher? Radio
love. You loved in this city? You read it in a book.

We know our best efforts are not for nothing. We are
necessary to literature. The ledge out of insanity into print.
Is thin and we make it with our lacerated arms our starry
eyes full of twos threes fours. Someone has to have a sense
of history. "Will you take your camera," we asked her. "I
don't know why I would," she'd answered innocently. "I
guess I might see some horses." So our haircuts against the
scarred wood go unrecorded. We cradle her, knowing she
will spit us back out in a form hinged to her own version of
momentum—spite. Still, it is better to be seen.

The train runs between a lake and a cliff for throwing things
off of. By a white radiator I found a grey cat, still alive,

moving in sideways humps, broken in the middle. I tried.
Her ferociousness tipped me away from interference toward
prayer. She didn't want human arms food water or an easy
death from a needle after a ride in a stranger's car. I mean,
there was the lake, there was the train. Do you hear me,
quadrangle of the human nest? No, they never hear me. I am
formed of what they do not hear. Reabsorbed, I would
scatter them like teenagers leaving small midwestern towns.
My exile binds them and their fictions keep me here, so I can
speak. She didn't want prayer even more.

I like the way the train letters or are they numbers flash by
at night and noise below and beyond I can still see the lights
of boats moving slowly on water, two by two. Three kinds
of travel, four if you count the fish still squirming in the
gull's beak, and four alphabets. Fish who have survived
impact report a sense of renewed purpose. Or destination.
I can hop a train by lowering myself from the tree that grows
through my porch. Ending up at Montezuma in my mother's
green pajamas.

But I didn't put myself en route this September to stop
myself among the ruins of romance. Among the barbarians
of the East. Is place stronger than personality? Is that why
100 years later they can call themselves witches and still be
roasting each other? The ruins hypnotize me.

Home, do they write in their houses? They don't hesitate.
Describing heads topped with hair or formal topiary gardens in black and white. They describe wrangling over
dishes and bikes as a form of meditation. Reminding me
again of the time someone shaved the horses. A bizarre
hieroglyphics, cantering around the ring with top hats,
smiles, dominos carved in their hair. Or Italianate houses.

Or spiritist circles formed around a dominant personality, incarnate or other, who wields a sharp instrument. A bizarre hieroglyphics, writing away in their salles à manger, their salles de bain, their salles à coucher, their salles à écriver.

"No women, never any women here. There have never been any women here…. What do you write in your wee book?" the train conductor asked two by two, unwisely.

Home at last, we re-entombed ourselves among the ottomans. We discussed the synopsis. We couldn't find among us sufficient positive feeling to publish two times two. We wouldn't expose her polar soul to our community. We were more heroic. We loved her, we waited for her return when we would try to raise her spirits while ignoring her gross tales of hubris, try to brush off the snow that covers her years among us.

Machines, like the kabbala, were meant to ease the anguish of the brain, its straining after meaning, its hopeless love and abhorrence of harmony. Impatient with devices, alpha dream machines, writing machines, creating conditions just as easily arrived at by accident or hardship. I decided merely to concentrate on the impossible: moving objects at a distance. Without words or devices of any sort. I knew a man once who claimed to be kinetic, as in Caucasian or pecan, as an excuse for not being able to speak the truth. Women, he seemed to think, were exclusively verbal, it was up to them. Two things joined, two things joined against the laws of probability. Thus ended a series of experiments begun 1971. A long experiment in various houses by water. I knew a woman once who said, after we separated and were trying to be kind by phone, "I've had enough of this little experiment." The joy of moving objects at a distance, their wordless float. Once in a trailer in Athens, Ohio, I watched a woman wrap herself completely in tinfoil. Until they begin taking up a pen or other sharp object, scrawling their primitive versions of physics on any impressionable surface. Dust. Sugar. Skin. Frost. I knew a woman once in Ann Arbor, Michigan, who went to bed each night entirely encased in saran wrap. Crinkling, rustling, dull dry rounded thumps. He rolled her in a carpet, he said, so he could beat her without damage. Once I knew a woman who had a body cast from ankle to neck. Lived on cookies and wine from the corner store, as far as she could hobble. We made movies every night. We made them without cameras. Once I went through a box of clothes abandoned by her former lover and found a lace skirt with the lining cut out, and a leopardskin muff. Protection is lifted. Speed is trapped. Women are bound and gagged.

I gave up my futile efforts to make the ether speak, the static, the aluminum foil, the diode, the extractor. I fastened on the idea of using the muff. It took three months of casual inattentiveness. On October 31 the muff could proceed by rocking side to side. She moved easiest, cold to the touch and vibrating in agitation, when I was furious about something or other. She learned to hold a pen between the padded folds of her lining and began leaving messages. pchhysom. gwpiils. Which mean nothing, but are amazing when you consider the means. One November day the muff rose higher, floated around the green room touching furniture and whispering sadly, "changé, changé." As I cried out in surprise and gratification, the muff levitated from the bookshelf and touched my face repeatedly.

The muff is sometimes overcome by a voice of bile whose acid spit burns through to the heart of her best intentions. She says habits of struggle persist like the worst kinds of images—giant crabs seen on a drive-in movie screen at an impressionable age. A line in the paper about a woman wandering in the desert after he cut off her arms. She says from where she is she can still give, wince, puff up, deflate. Take an impression. Leave a mark. She too strains to move objects at a distance. From where she twirls in the unconfined.

My name is Epizeuxis, but I call myself Race Track. Race because when you think of me I want you to think of speed, the only thing that holds us still enough to see each other. Track for the marks I make as proof of my existence. Race Track is ovoid and has horses, sometimes sulkies, everybody needs to have stories that begin, end, swell, repeat. I will try to explain. I don't understand myself though I follow daily all come loose eventually unconnected. Still I believe amidst a flux of opinions. A meaning will hold at least a few generations to ease my wandering. Patterns insist. Souls, like electrons, usually choose to be what they have always.

I started with three questions. Why does love end. Why does blood flow up. Who makes it stop. I am making a machine that will demonstrate. That will also be a perpetual answering. There is great need, I believe, though I myself prefer asking. Love and blood blink in and out simultaneously, that is speech. Otherwise you would never hear a voice just a solid noise that would become the same as silence. You so love your life that your blood beats in your ears like sinister voices during times of great fear or loss. There is a grand rhythm, a canter, three beat and b flat. Some learn to wield the bent tunes to become something other than what happened to exist. To choose not to be what they have been. New harmonies sound like discord from inside stasis. Words sound like nonsense, feel like bits in the mouth.

Some people want these analogies. Some want metaphysics. Some want history. Everybody wants meaning. They want you to lay it down for them like a railroad track. No one wants to wander.

I was a great healer. I wrote the names of angels on pieces of paper and tied them to a horse's mane. I could staunch the flow of blood by crooning but wasn't very good at exciting it to flow upward into the pineal gland. I was seldom tempted to bend a will. My failure lay in slinking from the repellent colors of so much suffering, mostly called love. I hid inside my cranium. I had a lovely vista.

Sometimes I think that's why I find myself without an amanuensis who would speak with the primitive muscle and echo of a throat, and heart, bending meaning, touching, clenching, never wondering where the voice that speaks so low is generated, warping it with want. I watch my body speed around without me, rapidly disintegrating. I have no one to blame for my meaning but myself. This is no channeling. This is coming to you direct. The pen moves for me. The camera photographs the pen moving with no visible means of support. I continue to try to answer questions. There's only one answer. Be kind to one another.

I wasn't, especially. Though it was part of my chart. I so loved my opinions. I still love the sound of my words colliding. I would have been kinder, but I was more disturbed by the deadening effect of comfort on words. I felt shock, in the long run, to be kinder than solace.

I am making a machine that uses a goat's inner ear, a mare's ribcase, a 6 volt battery, a diode, a 4 millimeter cannula, tincture of alkanet. If you don't love the sound of the words, you won't get results. I call it epizeuxis. It will explain your omens. Red and white, falling in flakes, dried blood and powder—portends your mother's wreck and slow recovery. Blood will flow back up into her ochre head. My machine will try to answer your questions, because I have to go somewhere now on a train. It will tell you why your lover left you, why one day she couldn't get deep enough inside and another day your flesh was her suffocation. Why a trailer carrying a four-year-old Arab mare turned over on route 23 going south. Bucking and screaming. Why they beat a woman's head into a discarded fruit, then cried about telling their mothers. Why when you feel most inviolate you pick on the custodian. Why once two things are joined, blue and red, rejection and arousal, henceforth you can't be moved by anything but purple, like a bruise.

Epizeuxis generates a visible field that has the property of thinking. Molded by the stark vision and intentions of the dead. What is resistance but perception? Remember when, tripping, your knife, hand, arm were stuck for hours in a vat of peanut butter? Separation makes bodies weigh more but mourning makes bodies lighter. Love makes horses jump higher.

Cars, driven by myriad anguishes, go faster. Numberless animal bodies are struck. Lifted and placed on the doorstep. Putrid and sacred. Corporeal and sign. In the place where I sit I am making you a spirit. I have to go now. Be kind, make room. When you think, be violent and intermittent.

Trouble Open

prose poems

Material B

bernadette

at the side rip the paper says WHET and CATCH CLOSE ORJUSTWARMWITHSEC. bernadette is facing away and making a pleading gesture. this was taken long before she was riddled. before she became a saint. we were in ireland; that same morning a man left with a heavy pink suitcase, hours before we checked in. four a.m., the woman said, and he never slept in the bed. she was terrified because her husband worked for the english factory. attempts to trap bernadette have failed. bernadette, people are searching. some go on their whole lives searching. manchester residents are advised to keep children and pets inside. sheriff's deputies in pontoon boats are stationed in the river in case she tries to escape by swimming. a private breeder in bad axe says even a declawed black panther can rip through a chain link fence. a disc jockey warns travelers on I-94 to stay in their cars. there is a four-inch print in the freshly turned earth. they'd give the world and all they own. bernadette.

if you say the word shoe, then I have a shoe in my mouth. this is how the trouble started. a disc jockey warned motorists to stay in their cars. it first appeared to protect her from the man in the alcove above the stairs. through a china blue veil she saw the cat, blue-black with an almost invisible pattern of words in the twilight. if you say a word and then the word

builds up on your tongue, spit as far as you can, but you spit
your soul, so please do not spit at random. they say the
terrain is well suited. women being trucked to work wear
veils against the word. five were found with a single shoe.
she ran after the veils and grabbed him halfway up the chain
link fence. his shoes remained in the link. I tell the world.
you're the soul of me. bernadette.

eleanor

coughing she remembered the word surrender. running down the road in her nightgown or strapped to the luggage rack of the station wagon the word had risen in her and caused her defeat. they were keeping her mail. they were giving away posters of the brinks women in the grass lake p.o. she was conscious of her dead father breathing in the kitchen, murmuring that he had come to like the art on her ceiling. the idea was to stare fixedly at the hideous brown painting of two dog heads up there and then at the word SHATTER. this is a picture of eleanor selling christmas trees when she still lived alone on the farm. she refused to stay in the room in the nursing home but wandered the halls wearing the required white uniform, paint covered, bitterly enduring her humiliation with occasional outbursts. "I'd kiss you but I'd poke out your eye," she said, sucking a straw.

ana

a fresh scratch, wet. we protect them. what makes a man.
cries and squeals. as he bent them. straight, five. a fear of
heights, fresh. we defend them. too young or too old. we
shelter them. begin to whimper while still wet about the
desert of their old age. begin repulsed at the curtain, veil.
cries and squeals. ick it covered me. she was, you know, less
famous. maybe that's why she did it. in that way, maybe I
did. kill her. wads of tar under her nails. expose, she said,
accumulating copies, days. what they called explosion was
her hitting awning. closer to home reasons for pity: too
young already shaped by shame sets a toad on fire. or too
old slowly rotting in a vibrating chair spare your fire. years
of reasons shatter sense can't cover cries and squeals of
kittens drowning in a bucket, a woman sliding off a ledge.

jane

vermont maid syrup and a bigger darker nameless syrup right beside. he's generic. even though the light's on him and her eyes are on him (the camera's facing him) a very private moment. he appears to be reaching across to show her how to hold her cigarette. he might be lighting it for her, but given what we know of him, he must be critiquing her personal style. she wears his cowboy hat. just behind her a radio three full cups of coffee, a postcard. the way her eyes are on him is wrenching when you have read the afterword. is this bias anymore interjected than anything else? bits of pancake glued to white plates. he's reaching across and the light hits one arm up across hits eyeballs down shoulder across arm reaching to adjust her cigarette, and ends on the side of her face turned to him as if lit by him. his pipe smoke a filter for the light on her head. is the third cup for the camera? why at the moment he reached? in the image as in the afterward, loyalty? captivity? this is still hotly debated.

laure

j'étais sans amis. without friends or I was his friend change two letters. the house has always aspect of unchange. mail comes my advance caused by these letters from twenty, wexford, poland. just as I'm never on the bronze plain I wait each mail to embrace space. your extraordinary timbre. bizarre script. I refuse myself there. still rubbing a saddle of old moleskin. mare crops on a little bank. I tell myself without end the histories since my birth to where I inhabit this word. curious moment when she knew angels were in the grain. what oscillates between these two, silence penance due them. saves she rises blue black and steamy. still between these two now by years when the red breath is was totally absent. why because we become parallel histories stretched punctured everything. this word work arranges nothing in my brain. I'm not poor and my new friend is employed by the race track. over all my father, his blue green eyes showing nature, what they do to prisoners. he says he has too much stuffed in his brain. wakes in the present night with the clue to the buick. leaks out. no lids. we have to help. great sweaty shape to throw against to subdue to submit to. there was a country full of love and leaking. dark wrapped car bales. knees skinned a black revolver $500 in the other pocket hot black cotton bunched and scabby. never enter this barn without saying the name and the condition that excludes all possibility of sanctuary that region may have had for you. never penetrate the reserve which determines you will meet your original meaning of shock and battery. never pronounce a single word. the region reserved in the alley or garage where necessary each meet our edge just to the moment when you can no no longer ignore your limit broken between risk and incapacity. profound hope born in these contacts.

st. theresa

insecurity in this exile and how we must walk here in avila.
the void has a great drawing room of its own. abandon your
equilibrium for its majestic turmoil, quicksand with intent
to nullify. no fear. greece glancing off a fish eye when I was
fearless, no I. someone pitches forward spewing fern seed.
for ends badly say unabsorbed, reducing all to a liquid. how
to treat them:

give them your fingers to play with. the insulation gave her
some advice. I have tried it, she said, the shock absorber, the
vacuum part. the outcry is still that I want to pass. that I go
to extremes. lose all thought. though she reads she can't
follow for her earthly consolations are of no interest imagining the intimate life of the superior corpse. perfect and
final indifference to praise or blame. impassively timing
beauty's debate, flipping cards from the back of the room.
are you a lover of horses? they asked her. the sort of question
they always ask. from semiparalyzed wear thin dense stuff
where snails dissolve the impervious with little interstices
as oil on paper filly's breath on frost.

the wound of look repays many, the odor of the other's hair
is a debt that pierces reason no deception here. increases her
devices so delicate, can't discern. consumed by favor knows

not what to ask. you may inquire, what more? I can't tell. it
seems she fears the heart will come out with the blade.
wages a fierce war. this time it is coming out almost
normally. it is sliding out watch for the cold as rapid as
evaporation of menthol. we could take her anywhere while
that is around her wrist. do you mean to permit of her being
taken to california? benefits resulting from this state of grace
are indescribable, knowing the malice of the world. takes
speech warmth resentment and minor tears. but the public
diminishes transport. there's a little something gathering
around. first the extraction, then the nausea, nothing gentle
about the operation, then the chill. a growing interest in the
solid fog of thought.

the blonde

car called me. right eye was killing me. said he dreamed he was pulling something from dreamed. she woke, said she thought she saw me early thursday morning. the door delaware his shirt fifteen year old fled to west indies a great old homemade and incriminating piece of evidence. he sees with him sons. I wouldn't embroider his shirt with his power of attorney. took, he brags. shows a mime of money. his cowboy wallet has just yelled at you. basement, pipe, boat out and sink it. earlier I come home with suitcase don't want to have to. septic system. definitely between all passion I think so by her intensity again. her breasts make a low soggy noise.

then I'm at a stable comparatively less in size, straw, two of hay. being a red stallion I'm of slight movement weight possible to lead them narrow. I lead them lacking qualities for years. then everything transacting in a limited way. they're going to mate in characteristic properties extremely slender fine as a voice horses names low as a voice. I hear people of low degree obscure in the barn a yellow firearm of small calibre.

he took up with children are so padded she faded outfit took pictures we moved all the mothers shots of an old her the

way he looks sketched. fine work this summer I say some
dock, take it out and sink it. she sees past saliva and is
worried about the combination. someone has a syllabary.
she has a knife. newspapers printed it.

fled to west indian upstairs, wood, evidence. I couldn't feed
her. smiling at the attorney. took off. yelled at the woman.
so I tell the cops. stairs, basement. the weeks mend. we're in
a room like a dance room. fact is vague. decide to get even.
I say "I liked M A R Y" now blonde and pregnant. I realize
I really don't night dance. night is force. I pretend to fall.
cops are outside. that's my name. wild, complicated. of
course at a pre-planned moment. hit the glass. the next
scene is a balcony. she says her breasts make a low soggy
noise. second floor inside mad as the path of electrons.
someone has told. I have a brief moment for years. a
pregnant blonde told us. then I'm at a stable, one of straw,
two of hay.

adelle

april 1853 is mere collaboration. Nothing more singular than the union of these two women; the one Natalie profoundly bourgeois, narrow, vulgar, and the other Rosa an artist more or less dishevelled with great talent an extraordinary life. running through the fields dressed as a boy crossed out or a horse fine boot the empresses award crossed out genius knows no sex (or wishes) gender knows no sex who would dutifully record the record come records own censor parent Natalie, a Positive Woman; Rosa a Dishevelled Artist, a dull, ordinary life

inventory october 1853 seven pairs of arms two pairs of arms of the son of recourse five camisoles of teeth four bits of blown perfume two for the hat two for the hair sachet of egg mint flask two sharp necks for the open robe three centuries for the summer dress one ivory ceiling

entirely in code december 1853 I came back I spoke insignificant things I was ravishing, astonishing, I had a dress of tulle I was incomparable I pretended to have come for the boat Rose. She seated me across from her son who fed me white cake saying eat for love (he la mort, I l'amour) I was embarrassed I ate a little. The maid told me sadly and shutting the door "Out to dine, to dine" then "gone, gone"

they she meant to say were toys all of this was a pretext
because of all the days at dinner they gave me marvels they
chose for me they made me eat it was a pretext then a game.
the maid tried to convince me but whose game?

turning tables may 1854 we who hold the table each have lost
a sister who are you? everyone cries where are you. light
what must be done to there go love so you see the buffering
of those you love. do they ever come back to france, are you
content when you hear your name, are you always do you
live with do you need them to come no but will soon yes. he
knows because he trembles your love perfumes the air of
my tomb the grave says to its exile, I am the sky.

echo

still rocks this hollow formed by heavy bodies who've
forgotten. how she shook. what to make of it. at the time it
made for recoil serious escape. a longing for the silence of
childhood with parents who never. did that. it shakes its
way through, her deprived. it finally reaches the mattress,
wet becoming rounder loosening an echo in my sternum.
why do they say in the region of? coy, as if they have lost the
specific stab. lost the place. he told me in the theater when
the man's head slid down between her thighs a row of boys,
the kind who've affected the look of jocks without ever
taking up a sport, all shouted in unison, making that arsenio
hall thing with the circling fist, "that's no place for a man's
face." the worst is when we fight about sex, she said. I feel
like a lecherous man. I feel like a cold man. we lie there
feeling like echoes of different types of men, not of course,
the type of man who moves on, moves an arm, turns you
over, keeps on anyway, despite, moving beyond your
initial deprived. the hair at her nape is damp as she sobs into
the mattress. it does have a sheet on it. trying to breathe the
sheet to life, the drowned bed. now I have to say we aren't
victims here. when we were short order cooks we wore
aprons printed victim to dispute it. I just don't think I can
enter the therapeutic economy. I can't bear that kind of
button talk. we're not victims here, though now we're lying

side by side with ice cubes wrapped in washcloths on our
eyes. its just an ordinary night. at lunch two businessmen
said "PMS has swept the office this week. I felt like saying
its ok girls, I'll come back in ten days." Ten days? They
always get it wrong. we left a tip but forgot to pay the bill
and the bartender stopped us. "did she do that again?" said
my friend, to make me out an outlaw. "dumb broads." I say,
that's what we say when we mean we count our irony as
riches.

cinder

brainfever, brain monster, how big a one can there be? she
asks, sleeping furiously. grey wool grey wavery dots but
silver water. going out by canoe or by writing a c in the palm
before lying down. real heron in winter retreat to literature
anyway. no faith in seasons or returns. or embers. glowing
a word for stephen king. fever a word for aids. also quilt,
boy, mission, pink, chevy. brain monster eating outward.
brain monster brain monster turns to grain oat grain fields
of ohio. horses where they aren't supposed to be. trample
memory. wheat failed to heal their sores, must be worn as
wounds as badges. oats are kinder but equally ineffectual.
drinking diner coffee she takes a monstrous pleasure in the
memory of a black horse, cinderella, rolling over. each time
add $100. terrible blue pie glowing like mercurochrome. on
the next stool he says he rolled her three times meaning the
truck called lucy, lucy in rhinestones on his leather back belt.
in the book she says simply, I rolled. meaning she caved to
her pleasure. only with momentum.

gimel

it's a stone wall or a piece of slate. high on the left is a rifle pointing off, draped with net like the other photograph of arabs whose faces are holes in the page, the one I call tooth. this one is called H A I. the H of H. a big H over the smaller H A I. sea of sea. an S above the A has been rubbed out. there's a small g floating above the rifle. having named it she can aim. chalk. it's hot. a troubled adolescent made it manifest. the H is on the left where it should be water, and the I on the right is right. the A in the middle where it is always posed, equivocal, equivocating, innocent. but the S has been rubbed out. or is it just forming? while it waits for the S to gather chalk, the A leans toward H which has moved closer to it. neither notice the I—sealed off in its own dark square looking rigid and startled, even outside the greater H. the rifle on the side of the inner H, with a river at the bottom and some trees for images. dust, pools of water, chalk catching light, no other earth. because G has no home in this century she is everywhere.

queer pull of things

especially green things. grasses plaited by a serpent wind
sinister in its miniature coherence. did they identify the
artist or the grasses' song? the particular waulk of bridey,
wife of callum, weaving him safe to shore. disembodied
now, confused but wild with energy at the whole field of
dartmoor hers to finger to spell. rags, bones, embers—
patrin, safe passage here, fellow traveler. before the date
when I discovered I would decry. I still doted on the queer
pull of things. nested buns in their powder box from off her
head when hair was dowry. I still kick myself, I could have
had them. instead, what did I take? crumbly pastels in long
shallow box, puckered watercolors of irises, macaws, me. I
don't see why she shouldn't hang around, hungry for
things, as I am. is a mind resident in a body anymore than
the qualities of things require them sitting in your palm?
woke just before she killed me again, strenuous nighttime
exercise. she has this knife. it pulls me toward a woman
whose ex-man took to a kind of mormon/artist way,
carving in the mountains knives to catch the eyes of veterans,
pushers, publisher barons in private exhibitions of new
york, detroit, l.a. they grew longer each year, just like
crystals, length having reached the length that dwarfs the
men who wield it, making their heads appear downright
dinosaur-like. she was driven. she was pulled. I of course

was guilty and so I pulled its point toward me through numberless accounts, frightening in their coherence, inexorable, plaited into one thick lash.

objects with qualities

we fought over this braid, hacked off at the neck, still furiously red, bronze, scarlet. our mother had severed herself from herself, we were pulled apart. remembered suddenly sucking and had to have white milkshakes with tiny straws. the queer pull of things. the popping noise as things leave this realm, becoming even more compelling due to distance and electromagnetic energy. a pair of green plaid boy-legged pajamas worn to kleenex, ironed folded in a chest-sized packet and handed down to me, which I wore as a mantel of protection in a world full of animal-torturers. a cat named katherine hepburn who had to sleep on top of the refrigerator. her boys, grown, would knock her down and suck. one became wild lived under the barn on hell creek ranch. the other, named gato barbieri, became puling, sly, dishonest. katherine hepburn, paws crossed oracularly, on the humming pear-green refrigerator. or any green plaid reaching from scotland down to kentucky across the river to ohio. the queer humming of things, laden with intention. right when you think, with everything growing merely longer, what's the point. suddenly objects with qualities marshal their forces. objects begin their advance.

news of its disappearance

reached me where I lay. they applied hot cloths. black beauty. eggshells. rooms in threes. its disappearance slowly reaching in. between dreams of white chocolate bark, wet ponies backs, then darkening. then a little thud, and the news of its absence lit the room with false dawn. nameless at first, just a hole. in a dream would be missing teeth, mouth a hole, or a car, brakes gone, rolling backwards down a hill and vanishing then the space. this is the place I like to trace. what chemical released or what word rehearsed turns horror to respite from it to its complete absence, the same word, that force that reckoning. news of its disappearance reaching me long before the meaning of it, what it was, how it felt, when I had it. its disappearance precedes its name. that's where I want to be suspended. a word so strong it erases itself—lover, mother, horse—once coupled with its sudden disappearance. the passage through which it burns its way, down which the news must reach into the carved out stinging place. anticipation of a hollow collapse. how horror (in a word) first carves then cycles back to fill it out and hold it back from caving.

low-grade fever

looking over the black pond, crouching, trying to lure the
swan with the hole in its foot (who spirals closer hissing
mad that it wants a wafer and I) strange, how many spend
their lives in this low-grade fever. when I'm angry. who do
I hear? you don't miss your water. when I'm sad I hear that
powdery voice low, imploring. til your well runs dry. I'm
a little pepsi now, I'm a little pepsi now, I miss my water.
can't stop missing my water. when I'm out, I hear the words
to songs turn in their ruts in wonder, to me, feeding me,
personally. I don't notice, I just call it hearing. overlooking
the perpetual water, which you may suddenly sicken of, as
with the word horse, tough luck. a perpetual low-grade
fever creates thought-disorder, malarial, only bluer-green.
spend your life in a low-grade town. backwater. I got plans,
I heard on the party-line, and they ain't for this little town.
who's there? hang up fucker. later overlooking the lake I
heard her again I'd know that voice, the fever, the hiss of
want. blonde of course. below on the black shore. low-class
accent, someone said to me once. the way you say pour—
pore. the way you say can—kin. poor kin, I said, obligingly.
when I'm angry I hear it anywhere but here, inside, where
it hisses. when I'm afraid, over the shower curtain a towel
slides off in its sleep, a sound, any sound within a certain
radius after a certain hour. since the killing. drumming bold
footsteps on the porch below overlooking the black lake are

my heart in ears, obligingly moving out there to make shape. when I'm sad I see fat men bent over into the mouths of cars and women with shorn maroon hair on crutches. it's all out there. a low-grade fever lets it leave, one webbed foot intending exit, but circle, one leaking water through an old wound.

guide, trample

above the lake on turkey hill a woman painted I have only one burning desire on the overhang of a crappy house. incest hung to it somehow. an astronomer, she left her post (like a gull vacates a slimy whitened stump) to move in with a family of mountain men. guide, trample. when you know so little you take what you want without morality poisoning syntax. your eyes are guided by stars your feet leave grass or children untrampled. fishermen below on the tracks become benign because you don't see their families. because they don't have guns. then they cough, at night in the dark. letting you know they never left. skim over them. a skiff, my mother calls a light dusting of snow. its a tender layer. trample it. I have only one burning desire, to leave it lying lightly, to leave no print. cover over. white flakes mixed with red are falling. I am plaiting a rope. frantic. climbing out of something bent and monochrome. duotone? red ink on a black and white photo? then I'm untangling the rope strand by strand. close up it's dark red hair. red and white fall like the secret of the OTO, only drier. trampled grass, blood, semen. blood! here is a guide. the family car, a black and white chevrolet station wagon, towed home, the passenger side soaked red. her head in the white bed no longer hers but a body ending in a football. with unshakeable conviction I register stitches as large and black as shoelaces. this dust pink rain, so comforting. the wreck recedes. the scar heals but the scalp can't yet be dunked. on the porch overlooking the lake, she dusts her hair with talcum powder and brushes out red flakes. it's all mixed up and I like it that way. skating a frozen winter surface where johnny hayward knelt and held his bloody nose to the ice. you leak, a white universe absorbs you. knotting it together. unbraiding a red caked plait.

where you slip out

nail hole in white wall beside green curtain. words won't come here they come hard. it must be a secret. does it close up if identified stranding you here with chicken carcasses and nameless paperback mysteries? on the page between the words 'gloss' and 'varnish' in a book about a book. there. or in looking far onto water instead of at the speaking face. have you ever slipped out into the face? no. horrible. stop that thought. it will close, the where, stranding you here. the whole point is the out. it can't be human. of course now you have to mention lilith, taking a tall green bottle of coca cola, a book, a blanket into the car in the garage. right when you were flying out of kalamazoo in a tornado, mother's day, prom night, medieval convention. town full of monks, debs, women without husbands, and the unemployed lining the empty mall, sighting elvis. one hour away in ypsilanti. she knew the unpopular son-in-law would come to cut the grass. vladimir, always the saddest dog on earth, cringed outside the garage door, in spirit, having died two years earlier. every time he broke something with his sweeping tail he punished himself by subtle means. now you have to say how she made things up. the story of her stay in hospital, rescuing a battered wife. turned out to have been a stretch in a straightjacket. says her daughter, lilith always lied. When vladimir was shot she bought $300 worth of books, all true life crime, the only thing, she said, that matched up with her inside.

sense, assumed

since a thing continues you assume it. guy interviews the
few who jump and live. senses become numb hypnotized
things. physics says impossible, or science. police send tow
trucks not police cars. all felt a sense of purpose rekindled.
gulls fly backwards in this wind. none, however, could say
what. I stood on that bridge in 1975. hearing pissing in a
river, wearing fox red suede. he said he saw a ball of light
emerge (she was knocked senseless immediately and
nothing) from the tow truck, push him over, then cradle his
fall (recorded of what she experienced in the dark roll)
found him floating, singing. eight of 22,000 jumped and
lived. when you have no sense of cold only wet no sense of
danger only time suspended, beauty, quality of light. gulls
fly upward. no internal injuries though they insisted impossible x-rayed. all felt a sense of pointlessness removed.
except for one of eight who jumped, lived, jumped again.
put her in a parenthesis. outside, now, gulls fly in place. a
sense of transparency and beating each cell a heart. two
years later and died. a bad sign for the state of the world? as
the guy concludes. or for women. a boa snake in newfield
has refused to eat for five straight years. no sign at all except
of her unique inexorable intent. better ask why he was
singing. kept alive by a formula invented by a vet. to
forcefeed such a throat with a rubber tube! djuna! maybe
she thought, what good is a *sense* of purpose?

thump and swagger

so inventive. the way it tries to reach. resist knit veins to maps bury eyes. insistent image rises not to be denied at least insinuates a color. wet slate. or drops out of a field of dark moving shapes horses grazing or wind chafing iron-weed. decide instead to pay attention to arousal, the focus that lulls the lying brain. leaks it. sign on a van says rent me, buy me. bunched wet cotton tank suit. three kinds of green pastel smudged together and lifted from paper to pads of fingers to forehead. smock covered in oils mostly the cool colors. any serious guarded look above a certain lip. temporary devastation. nervous smoking. the way she says come on. the way you settle in the saddle a little thump and swagger. the way she danced with her hair to tina turner at eleven. the way you say you danced with your doorknob. the way he held his upper arm when he saw you looking. her left arm stiff from an accident in india. the kind of hair when you push it stands up. the wreck, standing in the street, nose packed with glass, name shocked out of reach. well where is it still hidden under the words I wasn't paying attention I was waiting listening inside listing left. engulfed. cats, children, people, horses, turn away their eyes the only means to a little privacy. missed something saturn colored flung out of a deep green hilly curtain of woe. sharp reflection gone unrecognized. while something weaves its way toward the tongue, think about how she holds back, just then, just like that.

seconds before

seconds before the furnace exploded we saw a tiny plastic skull. which reminded me of my involvement. three other furnaces had been rigged. this one nearly killed my father. he was, naturally, the first to open the door. later I am shirking a man's robe, more lithe, more longed for than early adolescence, that confidence. are these the dream couplets of killers? who knows. I just read about them in the papers. how they are killing women with a speed unequalled ever before. what different thing rehearses us in our sleep? crime and its credibility. guilty as we are, we see no need for action? or are we really taking a lesson from israel? no, I think, not virtue. oracles stand dumb becoming decorative. does anyone dispute that we mostly wrangle amongst each other? I'm sick of women. I wish they would stop confessing. stop writing books. I wish they would admit defeat. go mad. go through woman to the other side. here on the other side anything is possible. what exactly? well, I might spit and hiss when spoken to, as I did before I was a woman, at the age of three. what from over here is possible that is not romantic? to have no stake. no pain of hopelessness because, no hope. no word for it. neither bestial, tearing out throats with teeth, nor dead, brain ice. something else. no looking down tenderly on all heads alike. no word for pathos. for personal. a lot of weather changes. I want you to know, it's really important. I meant to do it. whatever it was.

grenade

grenade got changed to pomegranate. I explode like a grenade she wrote. but decades later word isn't womanly. lesbians rewrite herstory. finding the history of a word excuse for changing her weapon into a fruit. digging her a second grave. lesbians who kill. as the falling bodies splat on awnings, linoleum, asphalt, faster and faster. who do they think killed renee at thirty-three? alcohol, they say now, digging her a third grave. maybe natalie killed her. women who kill women. maybe she saw a black smooth tarn where another, her lover saw drawers full of memoirs. maybe a vision of this bleak time settled over their utopia. still, when she said she exploded. she knew what a woman has inside her. he called his mother again, from paris, to ask again about his circumcision. "what was the name of the doctor? oh and I married that czechoslovakian woman. can't you find out? can't you call the hospital in beirut?" his analyst is writing a book. about him, he says. later that same day someone asked me if I thought she was dangerous. capable of violence, that is. his old lover who left his poems shredded on his porch in a paper bag. labeled "verse." this is the violence they fear: forty-five-year-old foreskins and an insult to the poetic sensibility. women who bear arms, aberrations, are kept in kentucky where there is never night. north for his murders will soon rise like napoleon after a brief rest. women grow hard, rape and murder of women

more common than circumcision. is she capable of violence? are we capable of restraint? anything unpleasant is
called abuse. hard we change the words to softer. I feel
assaulted by your nouns, the woman said to the woman
poet. to describe two people merely discussing carrots in
asses is unlesbian or unfeminist at least. merely gay. not
good enough. good girl is what she and her sister called
shitting. were you a good girl? today a veterinarian shot her
lawyer husband at their mansion by the lake with a rifle she
bought yesterday in woolworths and I want to know did
the clerk show her or did she get it from a book is it
something you learn in vet school? cheered by this I go out
to buy another version and a gang of boys jump from
behind a car "die, fruit. garbage." they still say carrying
arms will give us a bad name. draw fire. but I think of the
women in florida. they say the first to fall will be black as
usual. I think, only some. the first to fall will be fathers,
brothers, lovers of both sexes. I think how like fruit are
heads, bursting bodies. how like grenades.

white cabinet

all the doors of all the cupboards fly open revealing red. this, or I looked outside at passing cars. the walls becoming my purse as he saw it so I slammed, burned, gazed immobile down on metal moving in snow. from where I was I. for you to see what held appeal, well, impossible. become blind. feel your exile as a sudden revelation of nakedness. everyone stares at the creature, you tighten the small wet towel. someone looks sad. from where he was he could only see similar postures. anytime I straightened out of the frame. I turned my head away, there's always something else moving to look at. seeing went behind lids and surfaced as an occult test resonant with otherness, unwelcome startling truths, redolent with mystery, lying on the floor between all the things from ashtabula. from where he was he was bound to. mystery. little white cabinet, locked. mine was white but unlocked and with a red glass window, a door doorknob, a 43. inside mine shoe polish, shoe trees, shoe brushes softer than even the sound. but his grandfather wilbur's white cabinet. items without words. he can see but he can't speak. three small silver balls. no matter what in the kitchen the wife would leave it go upstairs when wilbur said so home unexpectedly from the office lock the door. insurance. to score a point I say sold insurance. mine made candy. to settle a score I take away the can't. then I have to take away mine. can't see can't move. so then we are suspended in

could have but didn't. my own wears a slim white apron is
pulling pulling pulling white hot shiny dreamy substance
over a buttered hook. he cuts mine a wad. she makes a well,
she pours in a poisonous red liquid from a small brown
bottle. she kneads. for the stripe. one cane weighed eighty
pounds and who guessed this won it home. someone said
those little balls don't really do a thing in there, how could
they, packed in like a cold tampon. but they hang a past and
a weighty silence. from where he was he tried to see again.
there it is. tried. couldn't. can we use failed? I failed my first
parallel parking. ok we can say he failed. he believed
penetration made people permeable. he couldn't see how I
could have, unless I couldn't not, like him. intimate. I began
to see a carcass in a row of them peeled, naked, but
bloodless, etc. I could agree. I could enter it as a butcher. eyes
open or shut. that cabinet. that cellar, that fort, that refrigerator hum, that boy. I could. but from where he was he
couldn't even try to see from inside me. try to seize a second
free of the push pull the magnetic strain the yes no it was to
be where he was always. there it is. that sizzling notion of
damage. so ennobling, so tenderizing, such a callous. he
wafted through rooms identifying objects later purchased
by wilbur: a green-headed monkey, sea-foam, an ivory
handled knife, a penis with a strap that was locked in the
cabinet. later in bed, would sit up under a rain of multicolored
candies that fell through the ceiling from above and disappeared by morning or arousal.

fox red suede

fox red suede coat with its lining in tatters. an item with a strong sense of self. suede holds long the imprint of love or idolatry. when the boy traveled to sing, the girl left back in the colder spring, removed the remaining strands, traced its phantom parts, cut new midnight blue satin. tucked into every lining were crumbs from meals where chinese fortunes may or may not be blank. a shocking new interior. a desecrated altar. no new object in the intervening years speaks louder. they shriek down the future as in a tunnel. the invisibles would say don't linger over trivia. men choose wrong because they have free choice. they'd say. I had no choice, he'd say, but see how much more interesting objects are in their unrelenting pressure, demanding presence, oblivious, impatient about all the moralizing. do you have eyes to see? that's all they care. tyranny of objects. try to find a line without its hook. the cop in bly's workshop for men to connect with the animus cradles his gun, and, on instruction, croons to it. in the sauna a woman from sweden says why are you talking gun? don't a lot get shot by accident? entering a foreign land. why do you always say men? don't a lot of women die as a result? the gun meanwhile lies in its heaviness knowing one shot not even heard just read about conjures either fear or vengeance in the heads of thousands. we think someone is breaking in. over and over someone breaks in and either he kills us or we kill

him. I tried it with a german shepherd but he got shot over
and over. now I cradle a midnight gun connecting with my
animus instead of his. the story hanging over every bed in
town this week and last has only two endings.

cloth so tight

wound my sleeping sister's hair in rags. warning us about
what happens when you don't know grammar. for instance
they hired the boy even though he wore a rope for a tie, he
knew grammar and heat, clothes so loose from arkansas.
while around him women stoop in clothes so tight. terrycloth
robe thirteen, white, three buttons. pressed against all
summer suddenly alive to the possibilities of touch. going
home still sexual and still then the death of it. sisters are
perpetually pregnant. this is the very bed. go on press it.
things that bind the mind. things of the spirit handed over.
tender coercion. things dreamed snuffed. this is the very
basement stair. where I invented the band of mercy. bandaged birds. hold me cloth so tight sheet presser in her
corner someone said they'd send us through it if we touched.
two dimensional as a page. coming for me, full of herself, I
remember to flatten. want things that bind and move.
things that strap. skirt of lace with lining cut out. girth.
choker. goatskin glove. like a mummy, only knows its once
shape by its resistance. cloth so tight your fury. cloth against
your pity.

Occult Devices

I'm in the bathroom cutting up her shoes

words not worn by sign or cipher. shelter, well, wood, templar. will shaken by touch so that set in motion widest stellar orbit. looking for a restaurant with the aroma of chinese ether or hong kong pie. its poor ground here or there. the upper level of a dim muddy barn where they bump. one dark pony I really want. the lower cool blue tiles. fountain has some confection they call clonnies. ecstatic lights on the horizon. kodak can't figure it out sends spies. they've merely placed us here together to deepen and intensify. electric baths sex fish making a bed in the river. a bird above her while he tells her. ringing, curtained lilies, steely feather.

studying what is close at hand

why look at a thing (inside of a cheek) to rob it. look at it like the gate it is. bats bald smile. circus life of the brain. that no repenting power can free. but studying what is close at hand. quit straining the air to be. she rolls her bandaged head and says perfume, and, resignation. won't translate to—the music wrench though it will it intends to where the dark sound issue and make light the walls to—infinite delay at the border. a divided head evokes from a hole in the ground no magic without or within sacrifice I meant sacrament. only a mark for a place (a crossroad where they call her The Rag) and when I said I put my hand in the purse and the purse was inside her I was innocent of venice but that doesn't mean purse was. I meant nurture cradle embrace enfold, border didn't mean to be wall but signal for the halt of breath to return to you vere the furry color of thought, embrace to set fire to transgress.

opaque dust lane

opaque dust lane that lying in the plane of its bluish
arms. burn a little differently. the light from this oval
patch of haze. sometimes those changes are dramatic.
grains, mirrors, the crust. semantics, astrophysics, the
lip. to intimate, don't call it. crevasse, don't do it. asides
are what sound so farfetched. what is or is not crucial.
what they were reading when they sank. steering you
through the midnight wrecks, a lengthy cut. shift needed
here did the part for harmony. astronomy. having learned
to look at anything with a vengeance. inner bark inner
bark. battery in all ways. we say this oh sure. an awning
used as hammock to catch the falling bodies.

numen conspires

numen conspires to the form of this where the machin-
ery is surpassed. refuse to submit. she held captive birds
named jasper and rose who chose her jewels. as pope she
bade them be still. a new color to poland, its roses and
cracks. in a voice of chocolate masses wilt. this hailed as
a measure of virtue. diluted. virgin wax, half virgin wax,
a little bit of bee in the oil. not only catholic workers shut
outside the hive and virgin and starved, but deaf. they
dance while pope unravels from the navel. the family is
threatened in mexico.

what some call numen some call volts. what you call sex
some call ectoplasm. small blue flame at its porcelain
post, dark blank bodies of cow absorber, hard at work
wherever you are. rain grounds their prison becoming
a thread. between cow and longer grass purple and
abundant. noise of the snap sounding down the lane
cow black between tyranny and upheaval. obliterate to
generate. wet weeks seek electric holes for their larger
martyrs. bees figure in the telling.

single blessedness knocks against the furry layered
bodies of the intruders. the shell button you bit is the
factory littered with abalone. green cracked window
long and slender by the river cypress root gave it the

slant. heaps of violated oyster. dim rain. indisputable dark. doubt? a table adrift and turning as language can't describe but can hint. disconsolate.

novitiate. the way a slurry sound hopes to hypnotize. harmony oozing its lethal vapors. where passion lay lies swarm all else skirts or admonishes. she lifting her leaves from her eyes in mock astonishment, tubercular, sunning. square but rounded violet well beneath your thumb. how I never finish. the perpetual ache in shin. replete. gardener's glove.

luminous ceilings

your fear graces another quarry. always cover your back
by floating down, looking up at the luminous ceiling of
sky through lake. your fear founders here. you ask to be
held and you are, shore to shore. you believe in imma-
nence. fear a function of future looking back at you in
particular. your crime there. three coral rocks placed
together on the railroad tracks. somebody knows what
you don't yet. going at dusk to pray for forgiveness in
advance or at least the return of the inexplicable, you
find: a board with a t-shirt sail nailed to a stick and a
candlestub in a can, washed up. inanna goddess of
water, vanity, someone else knows your name. ugly t-
shirt, something something fruit company. the bottom
of inanna vertical like the cliffs above straight down as
in quarry as in lost or trapped. trains whole trains bodies
suitcases never surface. inanna loves offerings made of
junk. she rocks her quarry, redistributing signs with
cunning.

mauvais radio

numerous small dogs attached to a blond girl carrying radio. attach end of wire to any appropriate electrical ground. diagrams show only grounds not practical, circus tents, masts, california redwoods. by screwing it into the plate over the outlet I reduce the nausea, head-ache, memory loss. looking down again on the tracks I see a head held immobile in a thing they call a torture cradle or witches rack or guillotine, forget. lanny told me when her sister had to get one she cut off all contact. I lost her then says lanny. her sister will say why would I want to see you? cradle will fall. breaks up the current of history. when men step on the moon, women's men-ses will turn against them even in commercial literature. who said this first, navaho, hopi? radio program on the birthplace of the blues. blue toothless rouge goes by below as the blond swings it dragged in three directions home. got me cused of forgery. can't even write my name.

sea's in it

someone watching the seasons, peat and water. someone smoking down to the stubs, rooting around in the
fire pit for butts. here she is, white blond head a hole in
the photo. red chickens black goats, the ritual essentials.
exile had its answers finally on that irish cow island.
through the unlatched window open mouthed boys in
their strangulated youth don't even know what they
yell. the sea's in it everywhere. then she's in california.
then she's in upstate new york. you're a long way from
home, said the freeville spiritualist. I'm coming to the
blond now. your black cat really misses you, he said,
meaning suky. with sorrow and such and a long shot, I
shall go into a black cat and be in san francisco. uncov-
ering backwards what is for longing after. that in spite
of exile no body home she still. calls says the plates flew
around but the fish in the home tank were fine. I could
have again lost all. even in exile an abiding tide. the sea
in every wave that rocks us together and apart. her
solitary island whiskey oatmeal potato. eggs before the
eggs stopped. because of course she sinned. if I had kept
my promise. but left alone to go into exile in the season
of animal, sea rust. no ferry. seldom any mail could
cross. brought a man out from Dublin and that was that.
even though he left at 5 a.m. married a man who works

in the san francisco aquarium. now her son draws dolphins continuously entranced by that curve of hope the way I was by the line of legs in a canter. police escort her husband to staunch the quake shattered seas of disaster.

false confessions

once the papers were brought to light. they proved the
falsification of evidence. I was one of the first. at a
crossroads I was shunned. books shut in my wake. I was
mentioned. my evenings—a clock face from the rubble
of grammar II on ann st., spray painted black from
behind in which I could be seen foretelling my own
theatrics. someone said I was part of a circle of witches
outside pinckney, michigan but no one dared. we kept
the menace cycling. mail arrived mauled and greasy
with a polite note from the dexter p.o.—"accidently
damaged in transit." on toma road by the abandoned
willett's farm I found a sinister wicker baby buggy. I
meant to speak of another time same place I saw a horse
beaten by four men in suits until he broke and took the
shape of a now famous indian leader. jacksonville prison
was not far away. we practiced nightly growing adept at
reading the words before they got inside and turned
personal. I was one of the first to take up rumanian
women's poisons. many were experimenting with daubs
of blood and mud but we didn't like the therapeutic
language of their method. we preferred to cut and paste.
listen, all of you spirits, from where you rest above,
swiftly with your knowledge. speaking your name can
be foul or potent depending on your intention, which is
to say your ignorance. I kept mine out of the news by

making my sex indeterminate. through a series of false
confessions. we learned to pay attention to fish with
rings in their mouths, birds with teeth, the smell of
burning wires, one lone shoe in the road, for all the good
it did.

my whole economy

my whole economy rests on rocks on dictated mouths.
words turn on me. any random evening an accidental
seance. a hunted face there in the black lake window
pane one boat lantern slowly passing through the
eyebone. I look driven. I look down. they're at it again.
dictations. they say to say: "alive beyond the call of
duty." "someone has to do it wrong." "undifferentiated
mess." a relief when they merely try to illustrate. now la
salamandre wearing the perfect wanton hair wheels
across a bicycle. that, they say smugly, bicycle basket
holds your entire sexual equity. now dirk puts two thin
fingers between charlotte's teeth and that has doubled
itself into their sordid vernacular for abnegation. abdi-
cation. abdictation. in mountainview, arkansas, and all
my hope rests there, a pen writes in a box. no hand no air
no trumpet no ancient baby trumpeting through. it's not
me, I say, exhausted. "keep the bale rolling" they answer
with one of the modern unstackable methods of feeding
horses. who could write over such demon noise? now
they are showing something they think only you can
see. the evil light moves over the body of a beagle. but I
spot it instantly, even though they thought they had him
curtained. this is a lesson in class or maybe travail, sigh.
the boy comes walking to collect the beagle over seven
dry ohio miles shoes no socks. I would say it broke my

heart, the beagle boy's trek, but they won't let me talk.
they say I sound like my father, would use poignant,
blister. they are shoving me in a drawer. my arms have
been amputated from elbow to wrist, hands sewn back
on, to shorten my reach. I can wave but not applaud.
somewhere further south the pen writes on without its
hand.

world wars might happen

do you have curtain rings? I asked the woman in the new town. world wars might happen, she replied. never having learned to tell the insane from the oracular. I staggered out under the weight of my willingness to believe. this machine measures the paths of bugs. their trajectory. the distances among stop, go, uncertainty. you can buy it through the mail. one about to be tracked clings tragically to a finger. every wavery line is speaking. and all of them say let me out of here. disguised as a man I said let me out. the minute you land you know better. nostradamus laid a track interpreted as 1992— the end. but he was wrong as often as the garbage man about the weather. the pen in the box in arkansas said relax. the world won't end in your life. you have other bones to worry. now I see my imminent demise every night on the news. woolworths might have them, she must have said. disguised as prophecy despair finds another target. as distance doesn't long for focus. distance is happiest. sparkling, cool, supplely muscled. waking from the concise articulate end of the world I found the words "squishy, kadafy or sadat." mother unnaturally blue-eyed waist high in water had been singing "we are going to the universal dome." as foreign as saudi arabia, her indiana, sect. trace its trail of slime. everything laid down is a code. disguised as distance I read read read. wear veils against the word.

Sound Worry

sound worry

worry wears away the cells inside her cheek. I believe I go
back home. every time I hear that sound. eats the coating
they all need, nerves, to sing in their beds. worry your head.
she worries the latch, unappeased by a blue block of salt. she
eats the wood at the top of the door. worry rides her
roughshod. come lie down. I hear that sound. an unsound
whisper, violent and profound. I believe I go back home. get
sick. take common medication. eucalyptus. rain on the
metal stable roof disturbed her greatly. she chews wood,
chews, in a lather to the knee. when they lie down, on those
fragile limbs, each limb a thirteen-year-old girl stiff with self
respect, then you worry. become unstable. come lie down.
I lie down among the complicated bones. worried. rubbing
her with rootbeer-colored liniment made of juniper. rubbing sometimes stops the chewing. sometimes my name,
soft vivid as loud. no consonant or edge or sound but
penetrating as turpentine. straight from nostril to brain.
pungent loss opening a sealed off tunnel to the other cavity
of loss. sudden and wide, ceiling so high. I go home then. I
smell her smock. the sleek of brushes. when, wednesday,
mercury, she too became obviously gone, the menthol
vacuum replaced her. becomes a great attachment. grief
takes its hollow shape from smell, sound, echo, worry. my
spectral benefactor. she paints I receive sound down the
long hall of paintings tipping in. I go lie down river. one line

leads to another. murder. nerves unchalked leap across from crime to crime. he floated, after shooting her, downriver in a bathtub imagining the mississippi far from the ohio. I go down. I fold. I hear my benefactor cleaning brushes, sluice, sluice. chew wood, worry my, our, confinement.

changing sides

as a child daredevil rider I did it indian style, one tip of a foot,
one tip of a hand, nothing else showing. I was a rodeo. this
moment a moth the size of a small palomino on the tree
outside. its frosted head parts blond against the red wet
wood, changing the subject. I am a radio. try to be here, now.
as if we ever are. the buoy swings, unlit now because it is
september. we aren't here now we aren't we, in september
by the lake, there. how hard it is to change when everything
is full of meaning, nothing is clean. I've already polluted
buoy, rodeo. september is irredeemable—friend, lover,
enemy, death of the lake body, smell of saddlesoap. smell of
fall in two places. immobilized by yards of gauzelike scenes.
wanting to change over and see my own approach from her
strip of tar, buses smoking beside, donkey singing dolefully
behind. wanting to pick up various lengths of ambivalence
and bend them into a shape I can wear and still move, still
ride. right here a cicada green and purple struggles to get
out of a copper shell, baked too soon for egress. I can't get my
boots off. I rode so hard. a new one, more horse than most,
she said. but here it is, september, dark, balcony. getting
darker. should I go in the water? would they shrink or
grow? but then they'd be more slippery. everything—
buoy, palomino moth, willow watching this silent ever
more desperate struggle with rubber. yes the rubber kind
for the calf high muck. where I found Friend hiding in the

pasture's stand of birches, watching deer. caught her with my hand in sticky grain. then practiced changing sides trying to get the right diagonal. balance. that's why you close your eyes, to feel. you can't be so busy always laying meaning. close eyes, feel her back curve up with the web of decent sensual things that come behind the lids, wet blue bark, red sweaty curve, perpetual silver green wave, and the words to say come here, night mare, come between us quick, save me keep me from changing sides.

forward desire

in his gold cutlass with his .38 and its swollen need to have
effect. his voice forward with desire, turning the word to a
bloodstain. shoots her through the chest. still at large. car
found in arnot wildlife preserve. blood clot they say for
women on certain streets. so forget about far away. there is
no where. not here not there. the senseless push and pull
that makes a horse go loco.

wanting coherence can either go numb or wild with fury.
gather your forward desire. are you looking with soft eyes
at a distance not a sharpened fence? can you circle away but
bend back without breaking? what did they say? they said
lift above bitterness to the wider world. but this is fiction.
film. christian science testimonials on her bedstand, my
candymaker, painter, her grocery bankrupt with imagining
and generosity. she died in debt still long after giving away
her shelves to the depression. she would rather have lived
but died in debt to no one. paintings strung along a narrow
hall. wanted that farm outside town in vain my mother told
me later the wants I never knew. they say not to worry
beauty eludes nostalgia. but not mourning. cellophane blue
is the ink over the sepia skin and the sheer lime green of the
fairy sticks roll them to make them thin and round. all the
layers become transparent. beauty opens mourning every
time. opens. her chest speaking blood. to keep you forward

in your desire in your desire to find him stop him. lift above
him too.

horses outswell our meanings for them with something
greater than nature or art. in art or nature get a glimmer of
their larger heart. her candies in all pastel colors of crayons
or bath salts. so you can. outswell this thing that speaks,
composed of almost nothing but stories of damage to
women, and resistance to words like damage. composed, as
you are, of evidence without coherence, bitterness, and
mourning. these are the spurs that shape your forward
desire. even as you feel it spring from a lake, love, a larger
sorrel body. how to speak. how to stop him. how to bend a
line that wants to exit into a supple circle wherein your
finest desires find more momentum. kill him first you think
and him and him. horses, invented for war, hate to step on
bodies.

strange corrosion

she's wrapping camera parts. outlined wholly against. her
own corroborating evidence. strange corrosion from the
cameras of the just. overagitation in the dark room. corn
sighs corn lies down. heavy are the cries above us as they
memorize our names, the ones they've given us, descriptive
of intention, into their offspring. two below, noted by crow,
rated as to danger factor, level of contamination. corn raped
fingers rubbed in satisfaction as I undid all of the hard teeth
into the bin. fall, fallen, october, for the horses. all the colors
of horse food with us here rim the sky and silhouette her,
photographing grasses. strange corrosion in the corn, black
rot strangely luscious. red stalks in the ditch. bittersweet
trailed the railing where I pumped rusty water crickets field
outlined against. stark black mare's image corroded by its
disappearance, carves itself on every subsequent want.

trouble open

a small strip still open looses its heat to gulls. gulls in trouble.
minus two degrees. seeking in a blinder way, one white
male haunts corridors. trouble shining. now the thing is
make a list. I have a list, he says, saliva glints, you're on it. its
circular he's at the outer edge. st. theresa's swollen vision of
the universe. she says a gum will swell or an eye for a day
then its over. deep sorrow coming finds a pocket for warning,
fills it, sending its agitated waves to point the brain in the
direction of trouble then opens and runs. stuff she calls it as
opposed to prophecy or paranoia, trouble or lies. merely
reading. lately you see loss, mourn, absence, vacant spectral
placed beside woman. he swallows his gum. he takes as his
hero montreal. he carries himself around in that febrile
man-shape, little projections, so poignantly unformed, those
sloping hips, so unequal to living, to opening. no one wants
to enfold it anymore, become putrid. white beans grown in
a closet reach long unformed limbs toward no future
seeded shape, growing longer whiter dumber in the dark.
or isometric. trouble open vein or fire. the earth bit her, she
said, rocked by the quake refused to eat anymore inside the
trailer. took her food, keys, leash to the square of earth even
though it bit. he said trouble open, counting himself among
it.

what rehearses us

napoleon, cleopatra. they've been here before but they've never walked on the railroad tracks in one body, one looking ahead for the heron, one covering the back for the train. what they don't eat you can live on through monday. for breakfast: yogurt, cottage cheese, apple, six grapes. she tells me what she had. she wears two masks for halloween: marlon, liz. her grey hair surrounding the butch on the back of her head the vamp facing front. every movement translates into two aggressions. beside us throbbing water behind us the long black steaming whistle. all her dreams, she says, are failed attempts. droll, arch, new yorker. but now her job is finding words for snakes shrews moles weasels stoats. the final mile before the salt factory shimmers marked by anonymous but specific maps scratched on pieces of slate. pieces of slate. pieces of slate. strategically placed. snake pressed flat on the tracks. slate snake rooms. snake feeders in every home. snakes answer every question cleopatra puts to napoleon.

I remind her of napoleon's mare. I always believed the more jumps you make it over under sleep the better chance awake. so why do three horses die during the running. the mare's leg shattered on impact. one had a heart attack, one fell over the stumbled heart. I know they ran in sleep they rustled straw big dove lids shivering in anxiety or self-

aggrandizement. to live in meat is to suffer napoleon says
not trying for comfort. napoleon, cleopatra are suddenly
everywhere. napoleon stopped going to the market. "I got
tired of watching walter fondle the zucchini," he says.
"jesus christ," says cleopatra. "are you sure it wasn't a
grapefruit?" I'm still thinking of the mare still jumping in
my sleep. suddenly a real crystal doorknob becomes visible
after three years only two feet away from the whole tenuous
arrangement (work, books, people connected by). so it is
possible they have always been with us. the final word to be
us. what fails to protect us. what rehearses us.

chew the bit

either you are lifted or you are sunk. the invisibles counsel
against this or that thinking, suggesting a slash. but I find no
comfort anywhere, least of all diacritics. I hear them arguing
off in the distance. jack has to wear a padded leather basket
over his nose. he ate so much wood he gave himself colic.
you come in there, you saddle up. the german girl rode him
with no trouble. everybody else. fear. he only looks far away
won't focus on a face. I know this. some know where they
are some only where they want to be. zorro is afraid of rain
in sheets. I'm protected from music. I walk past the stalls. I
stand by the hay. I'm standing there now. something, jack,
wants to crumple and flow. margarita doesn't do that, she
tells me, the best you can get from her is a chew on the bit.
she won't bend her neck. she's from south america. beasley
is too short for the distance between the jumps but somehow, maybe the name, he tries for you. chester loved to
jump. for every three-foot fence he cleared six. I know that
you lied. when you said they liked it. of anything. that was
childhood. I write as a veal calf chained to a box. with all my
rooms and clothes and no children to spend for, nobody in
the flesh saying no? even so I can say this. I write as a horse
in a tie stall. I don't even write to you. something in the chest
cannot focus the eyes on a face only a fence or the far
distance.

and we did

making up nothing. but what we did and how it writes. in the gap caused by tundras between speech and comprehension. why aren't you talking as the car drove us east. or I can't talk because you can't follow as I fall asleep back to the midwest. always two unparallel actions are noted. eery, mysterious intersecting barely touching strangulating charcoal loops like the man who drew blind on the subway carefully observing the no back contact rule. we did look at holes in the ground, ancient, october, invisible snake lined rituals pits now haunted by people on retreat who renovate puritan houses and paint their doors pewter blue. the distance between orchestrated mood and colonizers with no atmosphere of their own. playing music from the balcony, fingers attached to instruments below by strings. I did gaze on a face slowly unlining itself, on the blue green plaid folds of an open robe in that wrenching october light. copper leaves falling on a swamp. donkey skronking in the voice of both our fathers. how did we do that? so far out on a tarry night so far from home from the comfort of the indoor ring, ceiling rosy with dust, heat rising from horses all the colors of red. solid night before me could be the back of a truck no lights. unfamiliar german singer on the radio, going to you. making up nothing. making up everything secondary. I make everything up. often am left dangling in the poised and eager paragraph. dangerous doubling movement, to film behind the eye while living. a dream again where someone is kissing me but I'm looking at a screen two giant heads, kissing. can't take my eyes away. to look at the face nearby. and a voice says that's not love. but which? take my eyes. to have refused to represent, would that have made it sacred? they make laws against. to get the essence inside the actions moments then it slips. you're with her when she jumps or you're transported to another universe devoid of grace, you cease to live you write. and we did, love, she says. but sometimes said no that's not it.

tous ce que j'écris

everything I write is for you. I used to think I was napoleon's
mare. the heart of the whole insane operation. know now I
am napoleon. as well as the sweet chocolate shadow eager
to place your two sharp perfect forefeet precisely there.
everyone will wonder who. I intend exactly who I write,
after I see it lying down. écris de la mare. journal et notes
sans date. as napoleon I whipped her with an ironweed
stick, the flower still attached reverberating lavender tip.
my sister, I mean, not the mare. to make her ride the mare
I mean, or else we stood to lose you. our father didn't see the
point. I like to go about the world reading placards napoleon slept here and think, I did? then so did you. did we
dream about this page? were you stabled safe and dry
below deep and warm, while your brother lowered from
pulleys into catherine the great? the last violent encounter
woke me bleeding alone. napoleon had ridden me too hard.
or I had thought I was the great lying waiting to be lowered
into. holding your superior image never fails to get me *there*.
a tear or infection darkens a line to rootbeer down your
smoky arab cheek. a mon arrivé ici, tous ce que j'écrivais had
come to pass. I've made a special machine from the bones
of napoleon's mare with which to write. a pen, suspended,
moves across a piece of tympan sheet on top of a little stool
to the rhythm of the candles melt. it's important to remove
all human touch. the tympan sheet is the skin across my

chest as you write me of your willingness. everyday I write
you hard into the ground.